Natalie ~
the Scandalous Bitch
of All

by
Linda Spence Howard

Editing services provided by J. Scott Wilson
Copyright © March 2022, Linda Spence Howard
Wider Perspectives Publishing, Hampton Roads, Va
ISBN: 978-1-952773-55-6

contents

Chapter 1

Natalie was everyone's favorite girl, especially when it came to men. She knew how to take everything they owned, right down to their hearts. Natalie was every man's dream, but every woman's nightmare. She had beautiful black long hair that she loved to swing from left to right. Sometimes she would put it up into a bun, leaving two stringy curls on the sides of her face. That was her way of getting a man's attention and her inroads to their heart. One summer afternoon Natalie decided to take a run in the park for at least half an hour. As she was running, she noticed there was a tall brown-skinned man sitting on the bench.

As she slowed down from running, she began to walk at a sexier pace. Then she stopped and took out her sweat rag and wiped off her face. "Wow, it sure is hot out here today." she turned around while she bent over pretending to wipe down her legs. The young man looked up at her as he raised his head to catch sight of Natalie's beautiful legs.

"Yes it is." He was still looking at her from behind, now obviously checking her out. Already what he was seeing activated his imagination, "Hey, I didn't catch your name."

As the man held his hand out for an introduction, Natalie straightened up and smiled. "Hello, My name is Natalie James and you are, sir..." As water dripped off of her golden-brown skin, the tall man at first answered with a smile.

"My name is Jerry Cole! It's nice to meet you, miss Natalie." Jerry just could not take his eyes off of her. "Do you run all the time in the park around this time of the day?"

Natalie brought her head up to made eye contact, "Why yes, I do." As she finished wiping down her body, she sat next to Jerry hoping that he would notice her D-cup breasts, Jerry's studying of Natalie became even more intense with an increasingly warm, sensitive and sexy look. Jerry began to slide over so Natalie could sit next to him.

As the wind gently blew in Jerry's direction he picked up the scent of Natalie's sweet perfume. "May I ask you a question?"

Natalie looked over at him and said, "Why, sure, what's your question?" As she leaned her body closer just a little more. While her chest was directly in his face.

"Have you always been this beautiful and good looking? I mean, my god: you're sitting here about to take my breath away." Natalie just smiled, and right then and there she knew that she had him right where she wanted him.

As she turned and looked at him, she held her breath in then she let it out with a cool stream of mint-fresh air, saying, "What on earth do you mean?" She twirled her hair around her two fingers, and smiled. "Well, may I ask you a few questions myself?" as she turned and looked at him, "where do you work? Do you stay alone or are you with someone at this moment?

Jerry leaned way back and looked at her.

"Whoa, wait a minute, I mean, all I asked you is if you run in the park, not your life story? Now if you want to know a little more about me then how about we talk it over while doing dinner tonight."

As Natalie raised her eyebrow, with her legs crossing one another, she couldn't resist the invitation that he had just given her. "Well, Mr. Cole! Do you mind if I call you that?" She stared into his big hazel eyes. She started to think to herself, 'Well maybe I can get more than just dinner.' She turned and looked back over at Jerry and nodded. "Yes! we can go on a dinner date tonight. I need you to pick me up around eight and please, don't be late. I hate a man that doesn't know how to be on time. It just does something to me." As she cocked her head she caught him with her big blue eyes.

All Jerry could do was look at her as he got up from his seat. "You are a demanding little thing aren't you?" While looking down at her he began to walk in front of her.

Natalie smiled and pushed her chest out a little further as she got up from her seat and began to walk away. "Well, I guess I am. And I'll see you later tonight." Natalie stopped in the middle of the sidewalk. "Oh, and please don't forget to wear a tie. I just love to see a man that is well dressed and put together."

Jerry began to laugh it off. "Well, I guess I have to pull one of my best suits out, Huh." They both smiled at each other, and Natalie walked away thinking of how she could swindle Jerry out of everything he has.

Later on that night Natalie had started to go through her closet trying to find something seductive to wear. 'Now let's see... what I can wear tonight for Mr. Cole. I know, I'll just wear my little black see-thru dress. Or do I want to wear my purple lace one?' Natalie turned to her mirror and held both of the dresses up against her form. 'Well, either one; They are going to make Mr. Cole wonder what's underneath.' Her phone rang. She looked down at it as she picked up. "Hello, Tony, what can I do for you?" Natalie huffed a little while making faces as if she didn't want to hear the voice on the other end.

The voice on the other end started with yelling through the phone, "You know exactly what I want from you, and if you don't come up with my $50,000 your head is going to be on a meat platter, bitch!"

Natalie took the phone away from her ear with a look upon her face as if she had seen a ghost. "Oh, hey, Ted! I didn't recognize your voice, and yes, I know who you are – boy stop playing."

Before Natalie could get the rest of the words out of her mouth, Ted had cut her off, "look, I'm not playing with you about my money, Okay? Either you give me all my money or, like I said, your head will be on my meat platter."

All Natalie could do was hold her breath while her heart skipped a beat. As she put the phone back to her ear she replied, "OKay, you will get your damn money! And stop calling my phone like you have lost your damn mind; You don't scare anybody Ted. Who do you think you are?" She began to nibble on her finger while she held the phone away for her ear.

Ted had begun to laugh, "Yeah! You are a funny young lady, Natalie, you got heart, but you're not stupid. So where in the hell is my money at, little girl."

Natalie said breathily on the phone, "Like I said dick-shit, you will have your money by tonight." Natalie hung up the phone and threw it on her bed. "Damn! Now how in the hell am I going to get $50,000 to this crazy-ass man by tonight?" Then she looked over at the two dresses that she took out. Oh yeah! "Natalie girl, you got that." With a smile on her face she knew she was going to scandal her way into Jerry's pockets.

Chapter 2

As Natalie got dressed for her date she thought to herself, 'Now how am I going to get in touch with ...?' As her mind went blank she tapped one finger on her bottom lip, 'Come on, think Nat... What was his damn name? I didn't even get his number.' She turned and looked at her bedroom mirror. With a start she snapped her fingers together, exclaiming aloud, "Oh yeah, Jerry Cole! But where am I going to meet Mr. Cole at?" She continued in her head, 'I know I'll just meet him at the park like I did this afternoon, I have to hope that he remembers where we met up at. Well, I know that I have to bring my mace and gun just in case that damn Ted Rogers shows up.

"Well off I go!" as she turned to walk towards the door she stopped herself to and think, 'What the hell are you doing Nat? This is not you. You don't be running away from anybody, especially from some... wanna be drug dealer.' She looked at herself in the mirror and fixed her hair. 'Natalie girl! You are not in any danger; You don't have to worry about his little scrawny ass. Now go and have fun and get your free dinner.'

As Natalie drove towards the park she noticed the tall, well built man sitting on the bench. She immediately got out of her purple 2019 Ferrari 812 and stylishly walk toward where him. "Hello, is this seat taken?" She said with a lovely smile upon her face.

Jerry looked up and smiled. "Well no, actually I was sitting here waiting for you." Natalie couldn't help but smile wider absorbing his charm.

They both looked each other over, then Natalie held her hand out. "Well, shall we go," she asked, "Jerry, so which car are we riding in?"

As Jerry looked back at her, then at the cars he shrugged his shoulders. "It really doesn't make any difference which car we get in." Natalie turned around to see what kind of car Jerry was driving, and she smiled even harder. "Well damn! I guess we have to ride in your car."

Jerry laughed. Natalie turned and looked back at Jerry, and asked "How long have you had this nice thing?"

"She *is* nice." He emphasized, looked back over at Natalie and grinned meekly. "Well, I've only had it about a couple months now."

Natalie still couldn't get over how sweet his ride was. She turned and looked at him with a sexy smile on her face. "Aren't you going to open the door for me?" With one eyebrow up, "That is what gentlemen do nowadays, right?" As he looked up at her with those hazel brown eyes he gave her another smile that would take a woman's breath away.

"Yes, I will, let me get that for you my dear." As they both got into the car Natalie's phone began to ring.

She looked down at it, then looked back at him. "Oh, it's just a friend that wants to be worrisome." She laughed it off. "So Mr. Cole –"

Jerry turned to look at her from the side while driving, "Please, call me Jerry."

Natalie replied with a leaning smile. "OKay Jerry, so where are we going tonight, anything special in mind?"

"Well," Jerry paused turned his head to lookout of the car window, "I was thinking we could go to a french restaurant, or we could just grab take-out and go back to my place. What do you think Ms. Natalie?" All Natalie could do was twirl her hair around her fingers and keep on smiling. Since her phone kept on buzzing Jerry turned and looked over at her, then down at the phone. "Aren't you going to get that? It might be important."

Natalie took a deep breath in, held it and then let it out. "I told you, it's just one of my girlfriends calling me about her man problems. Really, she is going to have to wait until tomorrow." She replied with a look as if she couldn't care less.

As they pulled up into a parking lot. Natalie noticed the restaurant they were at, "Hmm. Why did you choose this restaurant? I mean, we can go somewhere else and eat..."

Jerry turned and looked at her with one eyebrow up. "Why don't you want to come here? I hear that this is a good spot."

Natalie looked around hoping that she wouldn't see Ted Rogers there. Jerry looked over at her with concern.

"Are you sure you're alright? I mean we don't have to eat here, no."

Natalie quickly looked at him, then down at her purse. "Naw, I mean... I think we will be Okay. Come, let's go eat. I am hungry."

As they entered the restaurant, Natalie looked around hoping not to see Ted Rogers. When the host addressed them to take down their table assignment Jerry turned to Natalie.

"Are you sure you want to eat here? If this place is making you uncomfortable we can leave right now."

Natalie turned, looked down demurely and smiled, "No, I think we'll be OKay..." she trailed off as she reached to hold his hand. Come, let's get our table, it's starting to get a little crowded."

They waited awhile to be seated, Natalie just couldn't help but to keep looking all around, then back down at her purse. Jerry caught on to this and asked, "... and you're sure you're going to be OKay?"

Natalie smiled, "Yes, could you please... stop worrying? I'm fine. As a matter of fact, I would like for you to place my order for me."

Jerry sat back thoughtfully... then regarded at her with a sexy look. "Oh... So we will order the same meal tonight then. Well, since you're having what I'm going to be eating, I think you're going to love what I pick out for dinner tonight."

Natalie just grinned as she knew that her money troubles were soon going to be over. As the waiter came to show them to a table Natalie continued looking around, then back to Jerry, "This is a wonderful place you have picked out tonight." The more Natalie would pretend to enjoying herself the more nervous she actually became. "Well, I think I will order some good tasting wine to calm my nerves down. Besides, I don't need anything heavy to drink. I *am* driving, and I don't need any more tickets in my life right now."

Jerry smiled. "Well I don't think you'll be driving back home tonight, anyhow..."

Natalie turned and looked at him sideways, "Oh? What do you mean by that: 'I might not be driving home tonight'?" Another big smile crossed her face. She was happy that he had said those words to her. "Okay, Mr. Cole, what are you going to order, since this is your favorite place to come?"

Jerry looked in the direction of the waitress with those big hazel brown eyes and raised one finger in the air. As the waitress came over to their table Jerry nodded over to Natalie, "What would you like to order my love?"

Natalie turned and looked back at the waitress, then to Jerry. "Well, since this is my very first time here... What would you recommend I should have?" With a little grin on her face she looked back over to Jerry.

He gave a little laugh, "Let's start out with a steak and salad with olive oil dressing, oh and a dish of onion sauce on the side. Also..." as he looked over at the waitress' name tag, "Miss, Lisa is it?"

"The waitress replied, "Yes, it is."

"Can you please bring us the best bottle of red wine you have?" Natalie looked excitedly at him holding her breath in as long as she could. She still couldn't believe that she had a gentleman with such good taste wine who was also a good dresser. She just couldn't believe that Jerry ordered her that nice meal just like that. "Are you sure you're OKay?" Jerry asked turning his attention back to Natalie.

"Yes, I just can't believe how beautiful this place is."

As the waitress returned with their food. Natalie gazed at Jerry, then stated, "I have to go to the ladies' room."

Jerry looked up from his meal. "Don't be in there too long. I wouldn't want to eat alone." He beamed at her with his sexy grin, then he got up from the table to help Natalie out of her chair. Natalie grinned back at him.

As Natalie entered the restroom her phone kept buzzing. She looked down at her phone she saw Ted Rogers number on the caller ID. 'Damn! Now what does his punk ass want?'

"Yeah Ted, what is it?"

Ted's voice rang out from the other end of the phone, "I hope you're having a good time, as much as you're wearing that dress you have on..." Natalie's eyes widened, and she backed up against the wall. Her phone almost dropped out of her hand as she continued to look around – back and forth. Natalie could still hear Ted's voice through the speaker as she turned and looked down at her phone.

'OKay Natalie, get it together girl,' and she put the phone back up against her ear. "What the hell do you want, Ted? I told you that I will have your money later on tonight. Don't rush me, bastard."

Ted's laugh crackled forth from the phone. "Oh, I know you will get my money now bitch, or you will end up dead. You have by midnight to bring me all my money, or else..."

Natalie leaned her head back against the wall. "Or else what? You know, I'm very tired of you're weak ass telling me what you're going to do to me. Like I said, lil' dirty, I'll get your money when I get it. You got that?" She hung up the phone, and Natalie put her head back on the restroom wall and closed her eyes. "Damn! Now why do I always have to be the one to be the hitman?" Natalie let a deep breath in, "Like I said, he's just going to have to wait."

She got herself together and fixed her makeup and hair. She looked back into the mirror. Natalie closed her eyes once more, gathering herself and thinking, 'Well, this night here should be very interesting.' She turned, exited the ladies' room and walked back over to where Jerry sat.

He looked up and stared at her. "What took you so long in there? I thought someone had kidnapped you." As he looked at her with a light grin up and down. She realized he was teasing, and all she could do in answer was just smile back. She tilted her head back swinging her long black hair from side to side while the light from the Chandelier shined upon it. "Well, I think we should go ahead and finish up our food before it gets too cold. Like they say; You don't want to eat cold food, it tastes very horrible." Jerry is held his gaze at Natalie with an adorable smile on face.

She looked up at him with a slight grin on her face as well. Natalie kept on pretending to enjoy herself, but knew that Ted was not too far from where she was sitting. She could not let Jerry know what type of girl she was at this moment. If she did her head would be on a meat platter. She realized she might just scare him off with the type of reaction that might come behind the revelation.

As they continued their dinner and conversation Natalie looked up at Jerry and politely said, "I think this was a lovely night. I've really enjoyed myself with you tonight. Maybe we can do this again someday."

Jerry looked up from his meal and started to grin all over again. "Yes, maybe it could happen, but only if you promise me the next time you won't be so uptight."

Natalie folded her hands and together under her chin. "Yes! I'll promise you, I won't be so uptight the next time we have dinner." She closed her eyes while smiling and shaking her head from side to side back at Jerry. As they both looked at one another smiling and gazing into one another's eyes Natalie felt safe for the first time.

Chapter 3

Later that night Natalie sat up in the bed thinking on how she was going to get Ted Rogers his money. 'Well, I could sell my diamond watch. Maybe I can get $25,000 back from that, it *is* Coco Chanel... Damn, Natalie, think... As she kept on to herself her phone had begun to buzz which made Natalie jump, then she looked down at her phone. Her eyes had widened, and she began to look around. 'OKay Nat, get it together,' as she picked up her phone and answered in her soft voice, "Hello, this is Natalie." The voice on the other end didn't say anything; All it did was breath heavily.

Natalie took her phone away from her ear and began to yell into it. "Look you little creep, don't be playing on my damn phone! Little dirty... As if I don't know it's you... Ted Rogers!" Before Natalie could finish her last words the call had been terminated.

'Well damn! Thanks for hanging up on a girl... if you didn't want to talk, that's all you had to say,' She threw her phone on her bed beside her. Natalie tried to think even harder, but as she lay back down her thoughts turned to earlier that night; The date she had with Jerry Cole. Natalie steadily closed her eyes and drifted off to sleep.

The next morning Natalie got up and went downstairs to fix herself some breakfast. Before she arrived in her kitchen she heard a strange sound coming from that room. She immediately ran back to her room and grabbed her gun. She slowly began to walk back down the stairs, gun in her hand. The noise had sounded a little strange, and Natalie had to panic considering that last call last night. 'Lord... I hope that's not that damn Ted Rogers in my house.' She started to look around, but it appeared that there was nothing out of place. Natalie yelled out, "Who's there?" but no one said anything. She proceeded slowly down the stairs; Natalie paused at the bottom of the stairs to take in and release a deep breath. 'OKay, Nat, you got this! Go on and protect your house girl.' As she turned the corner and jumped out into the middle of the living room, she let out a, "Was ha!" then wondered if she should feel as if she was in some silly karate movie. Nevertheless her eyes scanned around back and forth, all over the house. 'Damn, Natalie... there is no one here, but your crazy tail. He's really got you scared out of your mind. Well, at least I have Pebbles here to protect me.'

She glanced at her pink 9 millimeter. 'Yeah! I wish his little ass would come up here, and ,' but before she could finish her thought the phone had begun to ring again. 'Damn, Nat you really need to stop jumping.' She grabbed her chest, holding on to it as tightly as she could. 'Now I definitely need a damn drink,' yet picked up the phone with a pleasant, "Hello this is Natalie."

The voice on the other end of the phone sounded with pleasure and politeness, "Well, hello beautiful. I just wanted to call and say thank you for a wonderful time last night." Natalie's ear to ear smile returned instantly.

"Well hello, Mr. Cole. What a surprise. I didn't think that you were going to call me ever again after how I acted so paranoid last night."

Jerry caught with a pause, then proceeded, "Now why would I do that? I just told you how much of a good time I had with you last night. I was hoping that we can go out again soon."

Natalie's smile persisted. "Well, I had a good time also. So are we going out again this Friday?"

Jerry breathed heavily on the phone. "Well, I don't know about this weekend. I do have to work down at the police station and do some paperwork." Natalie took the phone from her ear and glared at it in her hand. She hollered at the phone, and then threw it.

"Hello, hey Natalie, are you there? Hello? Say something."
Jerry kept on a moment.

Natalie looked back down at the phone for a few seconds, and
then she put it back against her ear. "Hey, yes, I'm here. I just
thought I heard you say that you work at a police station," with a
slight and ironic grin on her face.

Jerry cleared his throat, "Yes, I did say that. Why, is there
something wrong?"

All Natalie could do was hold the phone and stare a moment,
then, "No, no... There's nothing wrong. I just never went out with a
person who works for the law before." Natatlie's facial expression
moved to surprised; she still couldn't believe what she was hearing.

As Jerry tried to continue his conversation about his work
Natalie took the phone away from her ear once again. She looked
down at the receiver, then back up at the mirror several times.
Natalie froze for a minute, then cut in, "Hey, look can I call you
right back? I just remember that I have something on the stove."

Jerry paused a second, "Uh... Yeah, sure," before Jerry could let
out any more of that last sentence Natalie hung up the phone.

'Damn girl! What the hell were you thinking when you ran
into him?' She looked thoughtfully down at the phone while it was
still in her hand. 'Well this is going to be an interesting date. People
are going to look at you and say... *Well OKay, Nat, what* did *you get
arrested for? Oh, I got arrested for dating a damn cop.*' As she put
one hand on top of her head and the other hand on her hip, her
disaster gesture, she continued that internal dialog, 'Girl, you must
be out of your damn mind to go and pull some crazy shit like this.
Natalie you have really done messed up this time.' The more she
looked down at her phone the more she tense up. She looked into
her bedroom mirror. 'Damn girl, and you were starting to like his
big, tall, brown-skin ass.' As she conversed with and studied her
reflection, her phone began to ring again. Sighing, she looked down
at it, then picked up the phone to answer it, "Yes, what is it, Ted? I

told your black ass I would have your money later on today. So please stop calling my damn phone."

Ted Rogers loudly cut Natalie off. "Bitch! I have your baby sister Jessica, now! I told you don't play with me or your head would be on a meat platter, right bitch!?" As Natalie tried to say something, but Ted Rogers started laughing through the phone. "Like I said Natalie, you got heart, and you're not stupid. So if I were you, I would want to see that baby sister alive and well. I'll suggest you give me all my damn money by five o'clock this afternoon, or you will be sorry." As Ted Rogers continued to breathe huffily through the phone a silence fell between them. After a few beats he began to laugh again, "Oh, you don't want to see your baby sister in the river now, do you, my little angel?" Ted Rogers laughed on in Natalie's ear until she moved the phone away and put it up against her chest.

She took a long deep breath, then, "Look, you ugly-head son of a bitch, if you even touch one hair on my baby sister's head. I will personally find your tiny ass, and I'll kill you my own damn self! You got that Ted Rogers? Don't fucking play with me! When it comes to something that belongs to me–."

Ted laughed even harder, "My god! You are a feisty little thing aren't you? That would be a good idea, I would love for you to do that Ms. James. Then, that way, I can dump both of y'all's bodies into the river. Like I said Natalie, you'd better have my money by five o'clock, no later, or you will find your little, pretty sister in a bunch of water."

Natalie tried to yell back into the phone, but Ted Rogers had disconnected.

Chapter 4

Natalie threw the phone down on her bed, and she turned around to look back into the mirror. "You son of bitch! I can't believe you have my little sister!" she exclaimed to no one; All Natalie could do was pace back and forth in her big purple, white and silver bedroom. "OKay Nat, what the hell are you going to do now? This son of a bitch has your little sister..." the more she thought about it, the more angered she became. She crossed the bedroom floor just a few more times, then Natalie turned and looked back over at her gold and white dresser and then into her mirror once more. She glanced back over at her pink 9 millimeter gun laying flat and looking pretty.

Natalie began to think more calmly and quietly to herself, 'OKay... Natalie, again, how are you going to play this one out without getting your baby sister hurt, but out of that hell hole he has her in.' She bit down on her bottom lip as she ran both her hands through her long black hair. 'Damn, Nat! This son of a bitch really has lost his damn mind; I mean really Ted. My little sister... Jessica... Over some damn money. What kind of man would stoop that low?' Natalie had stopped pacing the floor, but put her hands on her hips tapping them over and over again. She bit down on her lip a little more deeply. 'Damn! Now my lip is bleeding.'

She rubbed her finger across her bloodied lip. She tried to wipe the blood off from her lips with the palms of her hands. Then she turned and looked back into the mirror once again, only this time with rage. "He really thinks he is going to get away with this shit." Now she walked over to her bed and leaned over on it. 'Not hardly... I don't think so, Mr. Ted Rogers.' Natalie picked up her gun in her left hand and studied it, rubbing her fingers gently across it slowly back and forth. Natalie cocked the gun and turned around pointing the gun straight at the mirror. 'Not over my dead body he won't!' Natalie's whole body had started to tremble. She looked all around her large purple and white bedroom waiting for an idea to come to her. Natalie's whole face had started to look like a mad woman had robbed her of all of her name brand pocketbooks. Her phone started to ring again, startling her.

Natalie picked it off her white, fluffy bed to answer it. "Hello? Who is this?" However, It seemed like the more Natalie asked who was on the other end of the call, the more it remained silent. "OKay, you son of bitch, I know it's you, Ted Rogers! So why in the hell won't you say something. What? You're scared that I'm going to find your little ass and kill you?" Natalie took the phone away from her ear and slowly put it against her chest, then back at her mouth once more. Natalie started to speak into the phone with her soft cutting voice, "You guess right, bitch... I'm going to murder your little, short ass."

As Natalie disconnected the call a knock came at her front door. Natalie, still holding on to her gun, began to walk down the hallway stairs. The knock rang out louder and louder. When she got closer to the front door she held the gun behind her back, then she yelled through the door. "I said who is it?"

She stared through her peephole and saw a tall, brown-skinned man wearing a black jean coat with the hood over his head; he stood in front of the peephole with a brown package in his hand, but his back turned mostly towards the door. Natalie slowly opened the door, and she peeked her head out just a little. She thought this way, if anything was about to happen, she could easily, quickly close the door. "Yes, can I help you?"

The young man turned around steadily to face Natalie. With a big lovely smile on his face he declared, "Well, yes," He quickly looked at her up and down with big, brown-hazel eyes. "I have a package here for Miss Natalie James.

Natalie regarded him with a suspicious look as if she already knew who the young man was. "Well, I'm Natalie James, but I don't remember ordering no package. Who is it from?"

Natalie still had the door cracked just slightly open with her head barely out of it. The young man looked back down at the package and then back up at Natalie, still with a grin on his face. Natalie's eyes began to open wide with a little fear in them. She knew right then that this young man was no delivery guy. "Look, sir, like I said... I don't remember ordering any package. So, if you kindly don't mind, I suggest you take it back," Natalie went to close her front door.

Suddenly the young man pushed the door back open as hard as he could. Natalie stumbled backwards, but managed to still hold on to her gun. Natalie tried to point the gun at the young man, but he grabbed Natalie's arm and they began to wrestle over it. The gun fell out of Natalie's hand. Natalie fell, and they began to roll fighting on the floor. The young man leaned back and started pulling Natalie by her feet while she was trying to reach her pink gun. He flipped Natalie over on her back and she could look up at the young man face to face.

"What do you want with me?!" Natalie yelled, trying to scramble her way out from under him.

She was still trying to reach for her hand gun, but the young man worked harder to hold Natalie down and still. He leaned his head down close to Natalie's face, "You have no idea why I'm here, do you Miss James." Natalie stopped squirming and looked real hard at the young man as if she did not know why.

She leaned her head to one side to look at him out of the corners of her eyes; she tried hard to appear to look him over in a strange way. "No I don't, please tell me what is it you want?" The Young man lifted up his body weight off of Natalie and stared right into her eyes.

Linda Spence Howard

He began to laugh, "Ted Rogers wants you dead, see, there is a price on your head Miss James. Now, if I don't deliver you to him, dead, then I won't get any of my money that he owes me." He kept smiling down at Natalie. He laughed even harder.

Natalie continued looking up at him, "How much is he paying you to kill me?"

The young man thoughtfully returned Natalie's look with a slight grin. "A half of a million dollars."

Natalie frowned as if she couldn't believe what she was hearing. "Really!? Half of a Million dollars... and you want to kill me for that. Yeah right; I can double what he's paying you." She faced away and gave a little laugh. "You must really need the money, huh, Jermaine Spencer... Oh I'm sorry..." she returned to face him again. "Or should I say... Money Jay? I wonder why they call you that? You don't come back with no evidence, nor the money." Natalie stared at him with a slight grin on her face.

The young man, Money Jay, looked back down at Natalie with a look on his face as if he's wondering how did she knew who he was. "How the hell did you know it was me?"

Natalie studied the young man's reaction, and laughed again. "Now see, who is a dummy? Don't you know that he tells me everything?" It was coming clear that Natalie was bluffing – She didn't know anything, and surely Ted Rogers wouldn't tell her anything either.

Money Jay's eyes widened as Natalie used both of her legs to wrap around his waist. As both of them continued rolling on the floor once again Natalie raised her arm and elbowed Money Jay in the face. "Damn it! You little bitch, now I really am going to kill you." Natalie turned over on her stomach to crawl towards her pink 9 millimeter. Mid-crawl, Money Jay grabbed Natalie by her legs again and tried to pull her toward him. Only this time Natalie turned over on her side, and she lifted up both of her legs and kicked Money Jay right in his stomach. Now, when Natalie reached for her gun, she snagged it with the tip of her fingers. Natalie turned over on her back once again, pointing the gun right at Money Jay's Face.

She looked up at him and started to laugh. "Now who is the bitch?"

Money Jay stood there still, looking at Natalie for the next move, "Oh! So, now you're going to shoot me, huh?"

Natalie put pressure on the trigger as she pointed it directly at him. "Yes, I am going to kill you, and after I kill you then I'm going to kill your boss Ted Rogers for holding my little sister."

Money Jay posed a quizzical look at Natalie. "Wait a minute. He has you sister?" Now Money Jay looked at Natalie and started to laugh again.

Natalie pulled herself off the floor staring at him. "You really think this is funny, huh? And you really don't think I will kill your ass do you?"

Money Jay stepped back. "Now, wait a minute... I was just joking about killing you, and I didn't know he had your little sister. All I was supposed to do was scare you a little, that's all." Money Jay looked at Natalie with fear in his eyes. "What if we both get the money and split it?"

Natalie studied him thoroughly for a moment, then turned her head in thought. She declared, "Nope!" then Natalie pulled the trigger and shot him in his chest.

Natalie stepped over to where Money Jay's body lay with blood gushing fast. She bent down over him and spoke softly, "Now I guess I get your portion of the money, huh?" Natalie let out a little laugh with a smirk. She stood up staring at the young man as happy as she could be. She leaned her head to one side. The smile on her face had grew bigger and nastier. She realized he was still trying to breathe. Natalie sighed one big breath out. "OKay, you are starting to get on my last damn nerves," and she pointed back at the young man once again, this time at his head, and she pulled the trigger.

She looked him over once more. "Damn, I thought you wasn't never going to die." Natalie turned back around and looked all around her living room with the look of a mad woman.

The cell phone began to ring, and she pulled it out of her back pocket. Natalie looked down at the phone's screen. 'Damn! Now Why in the hell does he have to be calling? This is not a good time.' She answered, "Hello Jerry, how are you?" Natalie made pretence as if she really wanted to talk to him.

Jerry started to speak on the other end of the line. Natalie's face took on a very unpleasant look when she took the phone away from her ear and rolled her eyes. "Well, Jerry what's up? What can I do for you, my love?"

"Well, I really wanted to see you this afternoon so we could finish up our conversation that we had the other night."

Natalie frowned even more as she took the phone away from her ear again and started to laugh, "That's a great idea, but right about now I'm a little busy, but I will hold you to that date, my love." Before Jerry could say another word Natalie had hung up the phone.

Chapter 5

Natalie ran into the kitchen to see what she could dump Money J's body into. 'Damn, I don't have one single thing in here to put his ratchet ass into.' Natalie glanced over at the trash can, 'Naw, that's too damn small. What can I put him in? Ooh,' she smiled. Tapping her hands on her hips Natalie struggled to think harder even to decide where to look. 'Damn, a body shouldn't be this hard to get rid of. I'm starting to lose my touch.' She then tapped on her chin and deciding she was on the verge of something clever she felt as if the sun lit up her face. She tuned back to the room with the body deciding, 'Huh, I'll just call Mr. Cole back. I can tell him that I just had a break in, and there is a young man who is trying to kill me.'

However, as Natalie arrived back at the living room and began to smile to herself while dialing the call she noticed that Money Jay had disappeared. The man she had shot in the head was gone! 'Oh Shit! Where in the hell did he go? Natalie began to look all around the apartment turning desperate for any sign of Money Jay. How the hell can a man that's been shot in the head get up and walk away?

This time Natalie's overdrive thinking brought no laughter. What if he goes to the police or tells someone what had happened? Natalie started pacing back and forth again. 'Dammit! What in the hell am I going to do now?' Natalie began to rub her hands through her long black hair over and over again. There was a blood stain on the carpet, so it was all real. 'Ahhh damn... OKay, Natalie get it together.' She looked around the living room for her phone, forgetting it was in her back pocket. Natalie threw her hands up in the air. "This has got to be the worst day in my entire life!" she yelled to no one. As Natalie looked down at the blood on the carpet again and folded her bottom lip in to bite down on it. "Oh my God! Now this has gone from hiding a body to getting the blood out, and I have to think of something quick.

Yet again Natalie's phone rang – she turned her head to see where it was coming from. Natalie's eyes had begun to water up and she told herself to knock it off – this panic thing, 'You're supposed to be the baddest chick out here. So, Natalie James, get your shit together.' As the phone continued to ring Natalie kept turning around looking around for it. She began to yelled out, "Where in the hell is my phone at?" How can a small electronic piece of metal be lost so quickly? Finally Natalie stopped turning and began to pat herself down. 'Oh my God! Thank you,' as she pulled the phone from out of her back pocket. 'OKay I really need to calm down. She looked down at her phone then held it tight up against her chest. Natalie looked back down at it once more, resolving to keep it where she could see it at all times.

She answered the phone, "Hello! Who's this?" in her high pitched voice. She looked down at it for the second time. Natalie tried to recognize the number, but nothing came to mind. With no answer yet she got angry. "OKay, look here damn it! Since you don't want to tell me who the hell you are. Then I guess you should go and sit on a damn thumbtack, Ughhh, jackass!" Natalie screamed though the phone; The phone was silent. She held the phone away from her ear and just stared at it anxiously. She stabbed at the end button.

Natalie whispered to herself, "What the hell is wrong with these people these days?" As she tried to put the phone back in her back pocket this time the phone beeped with a text message. She huffed and puffed getting it to where she could read it. The text message simply read, "Your next." Well, Mr. Ted Rogers himself; she noticed as she bit her lips a little hard that couldn't spell "you're". Though she didn't recognize the number it just had to be him.

'If you want me so badly, then I suggest your little ass come find me yourself.' Natalie grabbed her gun and keys and headed towards her front door, but then she noticed some unfamiliar sounds coming from upstairs. She stopped at the bottom of the stairs and then slowly began to walk up them. Natalie put her gun up in front of her. As she got closer the sound got louder.

As she got to the top of the stairs she noticed that there were more blood spots leading a path straight from her bathroom. She took deep breaths in and out. Her hands broke out in a sweat. She edged closer to the bathroom where she leveled her gun right at Money Jay.

She looked Money J. up and down. "What the hell... are you doing in my bathroom?"

Alive, Money Jay looked up from the towel he was still holding to his face. "What the hell do you think I'm doing here? You're ass shot me ... twice! You little--"

Natalie stepped a little closer to Money Jay with no hesitation. She pointed the gun at his head again. With blood dripping all over her floor Natalie's face had started to fill with rage. "You just will not die, will you?"

Money J. looked up at Natalie and began to laugh, but he leaned over towards the tub. He stumbled and fell in. Natalie didn't take her eyes off of him, and she stayed aiming the gun at his chest.

"OKay, get up... Since your little ass won't die, you're going to take a ride with me."

Money Jay looked at Natalie in a weird way. "Huh? Where you taking me to. I hope you're taking me to the hospital, you little bitch." Natalie grabbed Money J. by his shoulder and pulled him up out of the tub. "Ouch, Bitch! Watch it! That's a gunshot wound there!"

Still, Natalie helped Money to his feet. She stared him right in his eyes. "Good, So hopefully I can put another in your ass. Now get up, and shut up!" She stood him to his feet with blood still leaking from between his hands. "Look, I don't have time to give you sympathy right now. All I know is that you're on my last nerve because your little brain and body here won't die. So I have another plan, and you're going to help me with it."

Money Jay actually looked at Natalie and smiled. He looked at her as if he knew he had this planned right from the start. "You know you can't kill me, right?" Money Jay held the little grin on his face. "... because I know where your little sister is."

Natalie stopped and turned around suddenly. She Studied him for signs of the truth or a lie. The more she looked at him the more tightly she gripped the handle of her gun. She knew that if she were to kill Money Jay then there would be no chance of finding her baby sister Jessica.

Chapter 6

She stepped forward to where Money Jay was standing with a grim smile on her face. "That's why you're going to help me take down Ted Rogers."

Money Jay looked at Natalie as if she had lost her mind. "Are you crazy? I'm not going to help you take down no Ted Rogers. Do you know... know what he will do to me if he knew that I'm trying to help you?"

Natalie put the gun right up to Money Jay's face. "You need to be worried about me and what I'm going to do... to you." Natalie turned around and gave Money Jay another unpleasant look. "Yeah, If you don't help me find my little sister. You won't have to worry about what Ted Rogers is going to do to you. You'll have to worry if anyone can find your body."

The wounded hitman took in a deep breath, "Look, all I know is that he sent me here to kill you and get his money back – that's all I know, but furthermore, I really don't think you need to go up against Ted Rogers, either. You do know he is a crazy man, right?"

Natalie was still looking at Money Jay – now ith her head tilted to the side. "And you do know that I don't give a shit, right? All I can care about is finding my little sister." Natalie went to walk away, but stopped in the middle of the bathroom doorway. She leveled the gun again at Money Jay. With a grin on her face as if she didn't give two cents in the world what even happened to him. "You do know... once upon a time I used to kill for Mr. Rogers, too, so... I don't think he's crazy enough to go up against me either," Natalie's smile grew. "So, what do you say Mr. Jay? Let's go and take that ride."

Money Jay stared back at her, stunned. He began to hold on tightly to his chest. "You are one crazy bitch, you know that?"

Natalie continued smiling, then sucked at her teeth as if she still didn't have a care in the world.

Natalie's phone started to buzz again. She took it out of her back pocket and read the caller ID. "Oh My God! You gotta be kidding me... Does he have to be calling me now? I mean, damn... I'm in the middle of something. I am really trying to kill someone right now," then Natalie calmly answered the phone. "Hello Mr. Jerry Cole, How are you?" Natalie still kept the gun trained on Money Jay, but then she waved the gun back and forth at him indicating to go, then to not make any sounds. Natalie's eyes widened while she continued to bite down on her bottom lip.

"Hey there, I was just calling to see if we could still go on that lunch date."

Natalie looked down at the phone and took a deep breath, "Well... I don't think I am going to make it this time around. I'll tell you what, though... when I finish what I am doing I will call you. You will be the first person I have that lunch date with. How does that sound Mr. Cole?"

Jerry giggled through the phone, "Great! Well, actually I am at your front door now. So how about it?"

Natalie took the phone away from her ear. "Wait, What? What do you mean you are at my door? I said I will call you, crazy." She began to look all around the apartment.

The door bell started to ring. 'Oh shit! Now what am I going to do?' Natalie turned around as she looked back over at Money J., "You had better not move or say a word!" Natalie pushed Money J. back into the bathroom. "Damn, now I need something to tie your ass up with so you won't get away." As Natalie tried to find something to tie with, the more she would get just frustrated. 'OKay, Nat... you can pull this one off. All you have to do is make sure Jerry doesn't go up these stairs. The doorbell kept on ringing. Natalie began to take deep breaths in and out. She looked down at her hand; She noticed that she had forgotten that she still had the gun there. She's started to think that if Jerry rang that doorbell one more damn time, 'I'll shoot his ass myself.' Natalie ran down the stairs to the front door. "I am coming... hold your horses little man!"

As Natalie opened up the front door, there was Ted Rogers standing in the doorway. "Wait, what? Where is Jerry Cole at?" Natalie tried to look all around, past Ted, through her front door, even using her hands to push Ted Rogers to the side.

Ted Rogers started to look around then back at Natalie, "Who?" he asked confused.

Natalie turned and looked back at Ted Rogers and started to ask? "What the hell are you doing here?"

Ted began to lean his body into the doorway, "Well, I thought I would stop by and see how my money was doing."

"Well it's doing just fine from what I can see." Natalie stared at him with disbelief that he was at her front door.

Natalie then backed up from the front door, while Ted Rogers stepped in. Natalie looked at him in a strange way. "Huh? Excuse me sir, but I don't remember telling your little black ass you can come in."

He turned and looked back at her and started to smile. Ted Rogers slowly strode into the living room. He noticed how nice Natalie's apartment looked, and he started to wonder if this was where his $50,000 had gone. He got a good look all around thinking aloud, "Damn girl, I just know I don't pay you this much money to be living like this."

Natalie looked at Ted with a face that said she wanted to throw up. "Shut the hell up! Like I said, what is it you want, Ted?"

Ted looked at Natalie sideways, as if she was crazy as hell. He slowly walked a little closer to her, still with his head tilted to the side. He started to raise his hand, reaching for her face. As then grabbed Natalie's face with his hands and got very close in looking as if he wanted to make out with her right here, in her living room. His eyes had opened up very wide, yet started to look a little glazed. He couldn't believe that his ride or die chick was even talking to him like that. "Who the hell... you think you're... talking to like that, Miss James?" Ted Rogers let her go, then stepped to the middle of the living room. He turned and looked back to her scowling as if he owned her.

"Evidently I'm talking to you, Mr. Rogers." Natalie leaned her head to one side. She rolled her eyes at him, then fixed Ted with an evil-eyed look. "I wish you would put your hands on me, go ahead... so I can cut your ass from here to San Diego. Don't play with me, I'm not in the mood for your shit. What is it you want, and by the way... where in the hell is my little sister Jessica, you creep?"

Ted smirked, then started to laugh. "Oh she's safe, she wants me to give you her love and gratitude." He laughed even harder

Natalie began to walk circles around him. "You really think this shit is funny don't you." When he stopped following her with his eyes she slowly pulled out the gun from under her shirt – then a loud crashing sound occurred in the direction of the upstairs.

That was the only thing that was had stopped Natalie from shooting Ted Rogers – the loud crashing sound. Natalie had almost forgotten that Money Jay was in her bathroom. She had turned and looked away, then back over at Ted Rogers.

Ted looked up at the ceiling, then he looked back down at Natalie. "Who else is here? Are you expecting some company?" Ted began to laugh again. He raised his fingers and gently rubbed them across Natalie's face once more.

Natalie grinned, "What – what are you talking about?"

"Is there anyone else here?"

Natalie leaned back and frowned suspiciously at Ted. "No, you creep, it's just me. So why don't you quit playing, and tell me where my little sister is? As a matter of fact, how about I just shoot your ass and see if you tell me then?" Natalie pulled forth the gun and aimed it right at him.

Ted looked over at Natalie, and he slowly started to back up from her. "Oh, so now you're going to shoot me." His face filled with rage, and he stared her down. "You ungrateful bitch. After all I did for you. So this is how you repay me? I give you a place to live, I also help you when no-one would even look at your little, dingy ass. And now you're telling me – me, of all people – you are going to kill me!"

With hate and disloyalty in her eyes she declared, "Yeah, yeah! Cut the crap, Ted. You keep running off at the mouth, and I am going to shoot you." As she still held on to the gun Natalie went to turn around and run up the stairs.

Ted Rogers hollered and lunged behind her, "Oh, no you don't! You're not going to get away from me that easily!" With a sneer on his face he snagged Natalie's long black hair. He pulled her back down the one step towards him. Natalie and Ted Rogers began to fight in earnest.

Natalie yelled out, "Get the hell off me, you ugly-head bastard."

The gun fell out of Natalie's hands and rattled across the floor. She kept trying to pull away from Ted Rogers kicking and screaming, but Ted pulled Natalie right back towards him. "Naw bitch, you ain't getting away that easy." Ted moved his hands to wrap around Natalie's throat. He swung her from left to right by the neck determined that he was going to kill her before she could get him. Through all this Natalie had forgotten that Money Jay was even still in her house.

With all of the commotion going on down stairs Money Jay had secretly gotten loose from being tied. 'Damn, I thought I would never get out of that mess. Now all I have to do is try to get out of here. First I need to stop this bleeding, but with what?' Money Jay looked around the bathroom for something to patch up his wounds.'Gotta find something quick, before she comes back up those stairs.'

As Money Jay tried to sneak out of the bathroom to look for something with which he could patch himself up, he could hear a lot of yelling and even glass breaking. Money Jay craned his head to hear something from the commotion downstairs. 'What the hell is going on down there?' Then he started walking towards the stairway. He could make out Natalie and Ted's voices as they were still going at it. Money Jay bit down on his bottom lip as he tried to ease the pain away. The more he really felt the gunshot in his upper chest. Money Jay leaned his head back and started to shake it. "Well," he realized from what he could hear, 'I'll be damned. She does work for Mr. Ted Rogers... this whole damn time.' Money Jay tried to laugh, but really felt the pain now. As he slowly tried to walk down the stairs, still biting down on his lip even harder to fend off the pain. With blood still dripping from his chest and head, Money Jay was moving at a slow pace. He started thinking, 'So now, I guess I'll get the rest of my money that Ted owes me – my $25,000. He got to the bottom of the stairs, easing right into the living room with Natalie and Ted still going at it. Only this time he looked down to see Natalie's 9 millimeter laying on the floor. Money Jay looked up at the both of them, then back down at the gun once again. He walked softly over to it and picked it up. Money Jay turned and pointed the gun right at the both of them.

Chapter 7

Still holding on to the gun, Money Jay edged a little closer to the both of them, then he whistled out softly, "Yoo-hoo," as he waved it back and forth where Natalie and Ted could see it. Then returning to pointing the pink 9 millimeter at the both of them. Natalie and Ted exchanged surprises looks. Both of them had to stop tussling with one another to looking up and see if Money Jay was going to be a problem; they they were in shock to even see Jay standing there, but for different reasons. They rolled over struggling to get up off the floor, "OKay now – both of you get the hell up."

Though Natalie turned to look Ted, she was still wondering how the hell was Jay still alive – and why isn't he tied up if he were. Ted Rogers looked back at Money Jay and asked, "What the hell do you think we are trying to do, you ass bucket?" Oddly, Ted reached his hand back down to help Natalie by the arm. Ted frowned deeply while beginning to look Money Jay straight in his eyes. Ted Rogers leaned his head back and laughed, "and may I ask what the hell are you supposed to do with that, shoot me? You don't have the balls to do it."

Money Jay regarded Ted for awhile, then he started to limp over a little closer to where he was standing. He stared down Ted and said in a soft tone, "No? Well, I'm going to kill you first, and then I just might kill her next. Now how about that money you owe *me*. If you don't give me what *I* want, your little friend over here is going to be my dinner for tonight. Now where is my damn money?"

Ted leaned his head sideways and looked at Money Jay in a weird way – as if he didn't know what the hell Jay was talking about. Nevertheless he looked right at Jay and laughed even harder. "You won't get it that way – by killing me. You definitely won't get it if you kill Natalie either, dude," Ted Rogers angled his head over to where Natalie was now seated, "no, but wait; you can kill Natalie – she doesn't mean anything to me anymore."

Natalie disappointedly looked over at Ted Rogers as if she couldn't believe he said that. "You son of bitch, you're going to sell me out after all the shit you put me through, and now you want to tell captain Rambo over here to kill me first. How about he shoots your lime-green, dusty ass first? How about that?"

As Ted Rogers and Natalie went back and forth with one another. Money Jay took the gun and shot it twice into the ceiling with a loud sound cracking thought the night. Natalie and Ted jumped, startled.

Natalie glared at Money Jay. "What the hell is your problem?! Do you know how much that's going to cost me to get that fixed? You damn idiot!"

Money Jay shook his head from side to side. "Look, I don't care how much your stupid ceiling is going to cost! All I want is the money he owes me!"

Natalie stood up. "Well, you won't get it that way; By shooting a damn hole in my ceiling, you ass bucket."

Ted Rogers turned, and looked at the both of them and began to laugh all over again so hard that he had to hold on to his stomach.

She turned to look over at Ted Rogers bent over from laughing, "And may I ask; what the hell is so funny Mr. I'm-not-afraid-of-no-one?"

The more Ted laughed, though, the more Money Jay got frustrated. He walked to face front with them to starts to yell, "Enough! Look, I don't care about your ceiling, and I don't give a rat's ass for why he's still laughing so hard. All I know is that he'd better come up with my $25000 that he owes me."

Natalie started to clap her hands at the both of them. "Round of applause gentlemen," Natalie kept on clapping her hands adding a circular motion. You both are jackasses, just broke the world's prize for jackasses," with a little grin and a roll of her eyes. Looking at them both made her stomach hurt. "Now look, I don't know anything about the money he owes you, and I really don't care, but I do know that my patience is running short here – and another thing," Natalie pointed right at Money Jay's face, "if you shoot my damn ceiling again, I'm going to kick your bloody ass to high heaven, you got that?!" Natalie turned around and stomped her feet at Money Jay as if she was in a parade. Louder and louder she yelled at him, "and stop bleeding all over my damn carpet, you idiot!" All Ted and Money Jay could was look at Natalie in a weird way. Had she had lost her mind completely? Ted looked over at Money Jay then back at Natalie.

Ted then started to ask Natalie, "Uhh... Natalie baby, are you OKay?" He didn't know whether to run or to scream for help.

She felt like she could run right through both of them. Natalie began to rub her hands through her long back hair. Just looking at the made her angrier and angrier, "Yes, I'm OKay," One could hear the sound of her teeth grinding together. Natalie's face took on the look of a mad woman who had just left the courtroom from getting a divorce from a cheating husband. She took a deep breath in, "but all I do know is if he shoots my damn ceiling again I'm going to kick his little head right through his damn throat." Her finger pointed at him with an evident shake. "Now do it again, I dare you!" Natalie's face was full of rage as she walked away from Jay, stopped in the middle of the living , then turned back around and walked right back up to him – this time, with an aire of politeness, she snatched the gun right out of his hand.

Ted cast right at Money Jay with a displeased look. He couldn't believe he'd let her do that. In his low-tone voice asked, "Money Jay, how the hell did you let her walk right up to you and take the damn gun from you fool?" He shook his head. "Wow! I really thought I had taught you some things, but apparently I didn't teach you a damn thing."

Money Jay just stood there with a look on his face. He, too, couldn't believe she had walked up to him with a loaded gun and snatched it. Unfortunately, this was Natalie James we're talking about here...

Natalie walked back to the middle of her living room floor with the gun in hand then turned back and looked at both of the Gentleman. "Well, it seems to me like I have my own gun back now," Natalie kept a slight grin on her face, as she began to rub her fingers across the pink 9 millimeter. She then looked down at it, and just a glance of evilness appeared on her face. Natalie looked back up as she pointed the gun back at them, "and now you two dummies are going to tell me – where the hell is my little sister Jessica? OKay, so start talking."

Chapter 8

Before Money Jay and Ted Rogers could even say anything Natalie's cellphone had started to ring again. As she took the phone out of her back pocket to look down at it. Natalie's face had started to furrowed up even more. She started to take a deep breaths in and out, waiting, hoping that it would stop ringing – so sincerely that she forgot that she was even still holding on to the gun in her left hand. Watching the phone Natalie started to panic with sweat beading at her temple. She shook her head from side to side then, noticing the men again, "Oh, don't think this is over just because my phone rang. As she walked circles in the middle of her living room floor Ted Rogers started to panic as he looked over at Money Jay, the latter began to pass out from the shot wound in his head.

Money Jay started to slide down Natalie's white wall leaving a streak of blood. Ted looked over at Natalie, then back over at Jay, and he pointed his finger – first at Natalie, then at the wounded man, "Look, he's going to need a doctor right fast."

Natalie followed the finger down to Money Jay, but started to laugh, "Wow, you gotta be kidding me. You want me to find his little ass a doctor... after you sent him in here to kill me and kidnap my little sister. Well guess again, Mr. Rogers. He's not my problem, he's yours."

Ted shook his head. The more expected of Natalie the more he thought she really had lost her damn mind. "Look... I know you and I are on the wrong foot, here, but if you don't get him some medical attention now he is going to die and it's going to be all your fault."

Natalie gave him another of her weird looks. "So, who gives a damn? Not me."

Ted walked over to Natalie, with his hands up, as if he was surrendering from a battle. "I will... vouch for him if he tries to do anything funny or starts pretending like he's up to something then you can kill me first, OKay? But just get him some help please!"

With the expression on Ted Rogers' face, not only he was thinking that she was going to kill him anyway – really knew that was Natalie's plan from the jump. Natalie studied him with the gun tapping on her face. She started to giggle with a little smirk on her face. Natalie leaned her head forward looking sideways at Ted with her eyes squinted very tightly. "Oh, don't worry, I was going to do that anyhow," Ted leaned his head back as he took a deep breath in as if he wasn't expecting her to say that. Natalie walked a little close to him and waved the gun menacingly in his face, "but first you're going to tell me: where are you keeping my little sister?" Before Natalie could get an answer out of Ted. A rapping came upon the front door. She turned and looked over at the front door, then back Ted and Money Jay. The former had moved his hand to rub his chest as if he was thinking someone would come and save him.

He knew that Natalie's crazy ass was probably going to shoot him anyhow – just like she had Money Jay and a couple of other people in the past. Ted was rather glad that someone had knocked at the door. This gave him a chance to figure out how to get out of there.

She pointed her finger at the both of them. "You two better not move." Natalie moved to look out the front door. By the time she opened up the door, and leaned her head out to see if anyone was there no one was. She shut the door behind her, and suddenly her phone started to ring again. She did look back down at it but got frustrated all over again, and perplexed: It was an unknown caller with a number She thought she had blocked.

Natalie scratched her forehead a little – whose number kept showing up on her phone. 'I would like to know, who in the hell is this person trying to call me?' She answered her phone with harsh tone, "Yes, who is this, and why do you keep calling my damn phone, you damn nut?" Natalie's voice had started to change to that of a mad woman. She strained to listen for the voice on the other end, then took the phone away from her ear. She looked at it in a strange way and then hung. She returned it to her back pocket. "Oh well..." She turned back to Ted Rogers and Money Jay. "Now back to you too jackasses," she wanted to circle back to finish her statement, but Ted Rogers had slipped out of the living room.

'Wait, what... where the hell is Ted Rogers at.' Natalie turned around again only this time looking crazy and feeling as if she had just left the state mental ward. She looked back over at Money Jay in a crazy looking way. She bent down, using her hands to shake his shoulders back and forth. Look here, Money Jay, I know you can still hear me! Where did Ted go?!" She yelled from the top of her voice. All Money Jay did was look at Natalie as he kept going in and out. "Look, I swear, if you two are planning to escape without telling me where you're hiding my little sister, then you two little shit-turds have another thing coming!" Natalie walked away to the other side of the living room, then she completed the trip to the kitchen in a run, hoping that Ted would hide into the pantry. She slowly tip-toed over to the pantry door and hoped that her sneakers wouldn't make any sound that would give her away.

Natalie threw open the pantry door and pointed the gun, but there was no Ted Rogers. "Dammit," she swore under her breath, "where the hell did he get to that fast." She ran back into the living room to make sure that Money Jay wasn't trying to get away either. "OKay look, Jay, we just going to have to leave without him, so get up and let's go. Natalie kept talking, but the more she did the more it seemed Money Jay wouldn't respond. "Hey, man don't you hear me talk to you? Are you deaf now? What, no telling me to shut the hell up or you really don't care about if I can't find him or not...? All you care about is your money... Yep yep yep." Natalie tried waving her hands in front of his face, while she talked at Jay.

Money Jay just was not responding. She looked into his eyes, but they were starting to look big and glossy – looking straight ahead. Natalie repeatedly called Money Jay's name as she bent down on her knees, still waving her hands side to side in his face. No, Money Jay still didn't move. 'Oh my God! What the hell did I do?'

She stumbled back over her own feet as she tried to get back up as fast as she could. This stumbling continued all over the living room floor. She started to crawl towards the front door backwards, but jumped to her feet as she grabbed onto the door knob. She twisted the door handle over and over again, unnerved. She kept looking back at him approaching a state of shock over the apparent dead man in her living room. She finally rose up with her back up against the door. 'OKay, Natalie,' she thought and rubbed her hands through her hair, 'what am I going to do with this body? I can't leave him in here like that. He's going to start smelling up the place.' Natalie stomped her feet twice as if disappointed. "Oooh! Why the hell did you have to die now? And where the hell did Ted go? Oh Man, when I find him I'm going to make damn sure I do kill his ass too."

Natalie was about to look around for her phone again, but remembered where she put it: in her back pocket. 'I mean, I could call Jerry Cole,... but his police nosy-ass is going to want to know how did this body end up in my living room... and I damn sure ain't got time to be explaining myself to no damn cop, not right now, no way. So come on Natalie, what are you going to do with Money Jay's dead body?' Natalie looked back up at the ceiling, eyes closed, tapping on her forehead with her fingers. Natalie's whole countenance had filled with fear as if she really didn't know what to do. The more she thought about Money Jay's dead body – over and over again – the more Natalie started to panic.

Natalie whispered to herself while leaning her head up against the back of the door, "Lord please don't let this man start to smell up my apartment." Natalie was starting to worry that today would be the day that her face would develop old lady wrinkles from all the frowning. 'I really don't need all of this right now, and I don't need a dead man trying to smell up my damn apartment like old fish.' As the thought came across her mind Natalie felt as if she was going to throw up. She immediately took her hand up to covered her mouth. 'This has got to be the worst day ever!'

Linda Spence Howard

Chapter 9

'OKay Natalie, girl... you have to come up with something in a hurry.' Natalie paced back and forth beside Money Jay's dead body. She stopped at the middle of the floor and tapped the tip of her finger on the bottom of her lip. With all the tapping and pacing her nervousness grew. 'Damn, girl, why can't you think of anything just to get a dead man out of your apartment. There's got to be a way I can get this body out of here. But how, how would I do that? I don't have anything to put him in. Or anything to help me carry his big ton-butt out of here.' One more deep breath in, then exhaled, and she put her hand over her forehead and rocked back and forth. She resumed pacing.

All she could think of was calling Jerry Cole to come and help her. 'Lord... I know this is going to sound evil, but if I go down for a crime, hell, I need someone to take down with me... but who?' She looked back down at the pink gun in her hand, but that simply made her angrier and more upset. 'Oh, don't you forget Mr. Ted Rogers. I'm coming for that ass. And I'll bet all my $50,000 dollars that I will kill you.'

The phone rang yet again. When she looked down at the number she had to smile with hope and joy. 'Oh, thank god a number I recognize.' It was her big brother Tiffany James. A lot of people originally thought that Tiffany was Natalie's little kid sister, that is until they actually saw him hanging out with her as a grown tall, deep brown-skinned man, with dark brown short curly hair and hazel eyes. All the ladies would go crazy over some Tip James. He much preferred for them to call him Tip, instead of Tiffany James. He liked to go by Tip with everyone, anyhow, but specifically it makes him feel like a ladies' man. Natalie answered the phone, "Yeah, what's up Tip?" in her low, scared voice, "What can I do for you?" Natalie tried to play it off by sounding happy and joyful, but her voice started to crack as soon as she picked it up. Tip knew something wasn't right just by the way Natalie sounded. Also, Natalie would normally be screaming through the phone by now. *"I don't have any damn money, so stop calling my phone, Tiffany James!"* If she didn't say those words he knew something was not right.

"Hey girl, what's up with you, are you alright? What's going on?"

Natalie's voice had started to change again, only with a high pitch. "No, I'm alright, I just have a dead man in my living room, that's all," Natalie tried to laugh it off, "and I don't know how to get him out of here."

Tip started to yell through the phone. "What the Hell do you mean, a dead man?! How the hell did you get a dead man in your apartment Natalie? What the hell did you do this time?" One could have heard Tip James screaming all through the telephone, sounding as if he was her father, from the next room. Natalie took the phone away from her ear. Another deep breath in and out.

Natalie started trying to explain. "Look, Tip, you gotta help me. I think I just killed someone." The phone had started to get silent all over again. Natalie took the phone away from her ear, and held it up against her chest, then she put it back up against her ear, "Hello Tip, are you still there? Say something." However at that moment all Tip could do was be silent. Natalie started yelling through the phone, "I know your red ass can hear me dammit! So say something. Are you going to help me or not? Just please don't say you're not or you can't, because I know you can. Like you said: I'm your big sister and you love me, and you wouldn't let me do this by myself, Tip," Natalie's voice had started to crack again, "'cause I really need your help right about now."

Tip had started to breathe on the phone, but heavier this time. "Yes, I'm going to help you, but you have to tell me what the hell is going on with you?"

Natalie smiled from ear to ear, because she knew that her little baby brother Tiffany James, wasn't going to leave her hanging on how she was going to get that dead body out of her apartment.

Tip began to speak again, "OKay Natalie, I have just the one question for you: I am still wondering why on God's green earth would you have a dead man in your living room? *'Oh, I forget, Tip.',* he tried to sarcastically answer as her, "... You're the one who killed him! Out of all the things you have ever done, Natalie James, this is the fucking worst."

Natalie put the phone back to her ear. "Yes, I killed him, OKay? All because he was going to kill me first. And plus, Ted Rogers was the one who sent him over here to kill me!"

Tip took the phone away from his own ear, then steadily put it back. "Wait, What? Come again, I'm sorry, did you say Ted Rogers? Ted Rogers was the one who sent him over there to kill you? Isn't that the guy you work for? Or better yet: isn't that the guy you said you weren't dealing with anymore? Isn't that what you told me, NATALIE JAMES?"

Natalie took a deep breath in again. "Yes, but that's not all. He has our little sister Jessica, too!"

The phone had gotten silent again until Tip's low-tone voice crept back with, "I beg your pardon: what did you just say? He has who's damn sister Jessica? Not my damn sister Jessica! He's really lost his damn mind. What you and him got going on over there doesn't have shit to do with our baby sister!" Tip started to breathe heavy once again through the phone as if he were a raging red bull. "You know what Natalie, don't tell me, I don't want to know, 'cause after I'm done with him I'm coming after your little red ass. Do you hear me Natalie? I am coming for you because you have a lot of explaining to do!"

Natalie leaned her head back away from the phone, "Excuse me! I believe that I am the oldest, thank you!"

Tip took the phone away from his ear again and looked at it as if Natalie was talking gibberish on the other end.

Tip returned to yelling through the phone, "You think you are the oldest Nat! You just got our baby sister kidnapped, you idiot! And by a so-called drug dealer! Now you want to call yourself the oldest, Yeah right, Get the hell off my damn phone before I say something to you that I will regret! Tip slammed the phone off in Natalie's ear. Silence.

"Hello, Tip, are you there? Please say something?" Natalie looked at the phone as if Tip was going to say something more. 'Damn! I would have to tell his crazy ass what's going on... knowing how he feels about me around Ted... Not only have I been keeping secrets from him, but I have still been working for Ted the whole time... after I told my little brother I wasn't... and now I have gotten our baby sister kidnapped. Now what am I going to do? I can't move this dead body out by myself – he looks heavy as hell."

Suddenly there was a knock on Natalie's front door. 'Who the hell could that be? I'm not expecting any company over...' The knock kept getting louder and louder as if it were the police about to break in. "OKay, damn! Can you wait a minute until I get my black butt to the door? Oh My God!"

As Natalie opened up the front door Tip came busting right through it, pushing Natalie aside then, turning, he pointed his finger at Natalie. All one could see on Tip's face was pure rage, "No, I can't wait! And I will not calm down! You're going to tell me what the hell is going on, and where the hell is this Ted Rogers? And another thing... How did he even get our baby sister Jessica? Talk, or I'm going to hang your butt by a tree limb, young lady!"

Natalie leaned her head back while looking at Tip in a weird way. He had flown past her so quickly that Natalie didn't get a chance to say hello. "Well Damn! Why don't you come right on in,

Mr. James?" Tip turned around and looked at Natalie as if he could strangle the life right out of her.

"Look, I don't have time for you and your shenanigans right now. Tell me where Ted Rogers is, Natalie!" Tip snapped his head back around. As he looked over and saw the dead body laying on the floor, "and who the hell is this?" He looked back over at Natalie while pointing down at Money Jay's form.

Natalie walked over to stand in the middle of her living room by Tip. "This is the body I was telling you about over the phone. I need you to help me get rid of it." Natalie waved her hand limply back and forth, indicating Jay. However, next she started acting like she never saw a dead body there before – certainly didn't have any idea of how to remove one.

Tip looked at Natalie a moment and then rolled his eyes at her. He turned around again to regard Money Jay's dead body. "So what the hell you want me to do with him? He damn sure can't talk – can't tell me where the hell Ted Rogers is, And he damn sure can't tell me where my baby sister is." In his lowest tone and seeming like he had flames of fire coming out of his eyes Tip walked over a little closer to Natalie, intimidatingly, "I suggest you quickly start talking, my little girl, or so help me, Natalie... I don't mind beating your ass in your own house." Natalie leaned her head back and looked at Tip as if he had lost his mind.

"First of all, I will be damned if you ever hit me. We will be some fighting siblings up in this house today. And second of all, don't you think I tried to get it out of him before he died? Hell, I even threatened to kill Ted Rogers if *he* didn't tell me where my little sister was."

Tip glowered at Natalie ever more. "And where has that gotten you?" Tip began to turn around in a circle holding both of his arms out. "I don't see no damn Ted Rogers, anywhere in this house! All I see is a dead man lying on your living room floor, Natalie. So I know, you couldn't have told him anything." Tip stopped walking around in a circle, as he and looked back over at Natalie, then he pointed his finger at her. "All you probably did was make a money deal with his corrupt ass, so you can get the off scot-free."

Natalie looked at Tip with water in her eyes. Weakly she replied, "Now wait a damn minute, what you ain't going to do is tell me what I did and didn't do in my own damn house, Mr. Tiffany James."

He leaned in even closer. "I don't care what you did, or what you told him. All I care about right now, is finding my little sister Jessica, and killing your so-called boss Ted Rogers."

Natalie looked back up at Tip. As she frowned shyly, "OKay... That's why, I called you to help me. So you can help me get rid of this dead body on my living room floor, and to help me take down Ted Rogers. So what's it going to be, are you going to help me or not?" Tip took a deep breath in.

As he looked back over at Money Jay's dead body. Then looked back at Natalie for a third time. "Yea, I will help you on one condition: once we take down Ted Rogers and his gang I don't ever want you hanging out with him ever again. You got that Natalie? And another one thing," as Tip held his one finger up in her face, "I need you to help me move this body."

Chapter 10

Detecting his subtle joke as only family could Natalie laughed, leaning her head back. Tears had come rolling from the sides of her eyes. Natalie walked to the middle of the floor, where Tip was standing over Money Jay. She patted him on his back gently like a little white poodle dog. "OKay, I was just playing – about helping you move a dead body. Remember, big brother Tiffany, I do the killing and you remove the body, OKay?" Natalie stepped back to look at Tip expectantly – this time without laughter. "You really think I'm going to help you carry a dead man out of my apartment. Yeah right," As she turned a circle with her hands moving from side to side as if she was in a beauty pageant, "with me looking like this, with all this glamor and hotness? You gotta be crazy."

Tip frowned even more deeply and glared at her. "OKay, Natalie! Don't flatter yourself, you won't that hot and gorgeous when you shot and killed the man. Now were you?" Tip turned his back and walked away, headed for the front door. He did turn back to look at Natalie as if he really didn't care what, or how Money Jay's dead body was going to get off the floor. "Look here, do you want my help or not? Because either way I'm going to find that damn Ted Rogers."

She took a deep breath in and exhaled the hot air, "Yes! Well, let me go and change my clothes. I don't want any more blood on these." Natalie looked back down at her top, disgusted about what was on it.

Suddenly, Tip grabbed Natalie by the arm. "Look, we don't have time for you to go and change and play fashion statements right now. All I need you to do is to help me with this body that's on your living room floor."

Natalie stepped back shaking her head back and forth. "Nah hum. I'm not touching that thing. And besides, he looks like he's heavy."

It was Tip's turn to take a deep breath in and let it out as a hot, frustrated puff of air. Tip looked sideways at Natalie and in a low tone rumbled, "If you don't get your hind parts over here and help me with this dead body you're going to wish that you were on a different planet." Tip pointed his finger directly at Money Jay's body, but looking at Natalie, "Now get over there before you be, lying right next to him!"

Natalie's whole face filled with fear, not because Money Jay's dead body was lying there dead stiff as a board, but because she knew her brother Tiffany James wasn't playing around with her anymore. She knew she was going to be next if she didn't get serious and help him lift. Natalie started to pace back and forth from one end of the living room to the other. As she stopped and cast a look over at her brother Tip, then an apprehensive look back down at Money Jay's dead body, she replied, "OKay, so if I help you with this dead body. What's in it for me?" Suddenly, now confidently Natalie faced her brother straight with both hands on her hips. "OKay, Tip, I needed to ask you this brilliant question: And where in the hell are we going to put it?"

Tip grinned. "Know what? You are one piece of work. You leave that up to me. All I need you to do is just help me carry his body to the car. Can you do that?"

Natalie went to bend down to grab Money Jay's legs, but then straightened back up, her expression changed again. "And who the hell car are you going to put him in?" Natalie's eyes widened, her face tightened and she clenched her teeth, "I hope like hell not my damn car." She had a visible flash of anger, "No, you gotta be crazy Tip. I just got that car. Do you know how much that car cost me?" She still looked at Tiffany as if he had lost his mind. "Hell No! I will be damned if we put a dead body in my brand new car... And besides... Why can't we put him in your car? You don't have a newer one, anyway."

Tip had been bending to lift as well, but stopped to look back at Natalie as if he wanted to strangle her. "You do know you're getting on my last damn nerve, right? As debating with Natalie kept right on going , Tip's hands started to form into a shape as if they had arthritis in them – the shape of her neck. Tip pointed his finger at Natalie again. "I really don't care what you say, he's going in your damn car if you like or not, Miss Fashionable. Oooh, you are so dead, after we get this body out of here!"

Natalie's eyes widened even more. She walked to the other side of the living room and looked Tip up and down as if he had really lost his damn mind. She thought to herself, 'Yeah, I need to put his butt in the nuthouse after all this is over.' Natalie walked a little closer to Tip. "OKay, OKay! I will go into the kitchen and find some big trash bags to put his body in. Damn! You starting to get on my damn nerves you know that, Tiffany James." this last Natalie yelled back as she started walking to the kitchen, "And you hope I still have some left in there. If not you're going to have to carry him out in your hands, *punk*!"

Tip hung his head and shook it slowly side to side. When she arrived into the kitchen she looked around as if she didn't know where anything was. 'Oh my God, where are those trash bags?' Natalie looked all around the kitchen: bottom cabinets, top cabinets, top of cabinets... 'Wow, now I can't even find anything to put my evidence in. Damn Nat, you sure know how to be a badass, but you can't even find one trash bag in your own house. What kind of hit woman are you if you can't get rid of someone? OKay, Natalie you better get something quick – you don't want him to start smelling up the place.'

Tip, noticing how long this was taking yelled from the living room to the kitchen, "Hey girl, what's taking you so long in there?

What... I know you didn't have to make the garbage bags, did you? Natalie, Come on here, we don't have all day!"

Natalie yelled back, "OKay! I'm coming, and stop rushing me. I'm going as fast as I can, Mr. Tiffany." She walked politely back into the living room and stopped to look at Tip as if she wanted to hang him by both of his feet. She then walked over to the couch where she proceeded to lay her entire body down as if it was her queen sized bed. Natalie barely raised her head to look over at Tip. She squinted her eyes a little tighter, thinking hard, 'Natalie, how we gonna get this body out of my living room without my big head brother trying to boss me around.' At this moment Natalie felt like she had no time to argue back and forth with Tip. All she wanted to do was move that dead body out of her apartment. Looking at Tip was just making her upset. Spoontaineously she sat straight up on the sofa and yelled out at Tip, "I know one thing that you're going to do Mr., is stop fucking bossing me around!" Natalie pointed at the front door, "No! You're going to find yourself outside sir!"

Tip looked at her in a strange way, his head leaning like a confused puppy. "Umm... Nat where are the trash bags?" Tip shoved his shoulders up and down. Really he didn't care two cents about what Natalie was saying.

Natalie raised her head up once more to look over at Tip. "Where I left them at, in the Damn store! As a matter of fact why don't you go and get them?" Natalie took her finger and pointed it right at Tiffany. "Since you *are* in charge of everything Mr. James."

Tip shook his head once more, now he knew she had lost her entire mind.

He walked over to the sofa, grabbed Natalie and shoved her completely onto the floor. "No! I don't want to go to no damn store and get no trash bags. Technically I'm only here to help you, noble fashion queen! Don't you have any old sheets or a duffel bag laying around here, somewhere in the $5000 a month condo?!"

Linda Spence Howard

Natalie jumped up from the floor fast. She looked back over her shoulder at Tip and yelled out, "Hell no, I don't have any old sheets or any duffel bags!" Natalie crossed her arms. "Do you know how much do my sheets and duffel bag cost me?"

Tip leaned his head back as he threw his hands over his face – so frustrated! "No, I don't know and I don't care, but I do know that you're going to give me something to put this body in, or I'm going out of the front door! Girl, you're going to stop playing with me. It's not the place, and this *damn* sure ain't the time," he walked over by the front door, a little grin on his face, "...oh, and Natalie, if I was you I would try and hurry up and find something to put this dead body in before you end up in something just like ... whatever it is."

"Well" I think I'll go and get you them sheets now, like you asked for." She eased her way down the hallway hoping that her baby brother wouldn't try and pop her head off her body.

Chapter 11

Natalie ran up the stairs and pretended like she was looking for new Kate Spade designer duffel bag – as if she really wanted to put a dead body into it. Natalie loved her designer bags and would kill for a name brand designer if she had to. At the top of the stairs she looked around, then she looked back down the stairs see if sure that her crazy, delusional brother was coming. She ran straight into her bedroom and locked the door. Natalie leaned her back against the door and clutched her chest and her head at the same time. She walked over and looked into her bedroom mirror, pulled back her long black hair and tucked it behind her eartried relaxing her hold on to her chest to release the panic. So scared that she had to fight the impetus to breathe heavily. 'Oh my God, this brother of mine is really crazy. I mean, he got me were I can't even breathe right.' As she put her head down and closed her eyes Natalie took in two big breaths and exhaled them out slowly. She raised her head up again and to face herself in the mirror. 'OKay Nat, you got this girl. All you have to do is march yourself back down them stairs, and you tell him that you're not putting no dead body into none of your good designer bags – whether he likes it or not.' Natalie was still looking at the mirror and held onto the dresser as tight as she could grip it. Natalie looked over at her closet and then back at herself. As she thought and confronted her reflection, 'Natalie this is going to be one long night,' Tip yelled from the bottom of the stairs .

"OKay, girl, what in the hell are you up there doing?! I know you're not hiding, are you?!"

Natalie opened up her bedroom door, and yelled back. "No, you damn jerk! I'm still looking for the bag, if you don't mind. As of matter of fact, how about you go and look for the bags yourself? Can you do that for a change instead of bossing people around Mr. I'm-in-charge?"

Linda Spence Howard

Tip yelleded back again, "Look, you need to hurry up, it won't be long before this body starts to smell down here!"

Natalie turned her head quickly, as her eyes widened. "Oh hell naw, I can't have no dead body smelling up my damn condo." She ran over to the closet and grabbed one of her old Nike duffel bags. As she held the bag in the air Naltalie looked at it in with an odd expression. While leaning her head back she started to shake it. Looking at the bag in her left hand, she thought it should do for now and ran straight out of her bedroom doorway and down the stairs to hand it to Tip. "OKay Tiffany James, you old me a new duffel bag, and I don't want no cheap one either. You got that?"

Tip looked incredulously at Natalie as if she had lost her last mind. "Girl, if you don't leave me the hell alone about a name brand duffel bag I'm going to strangle you." Tip stepped to the middle of the floor, bending down to position Money Jay's lifeless form. Tip pointed his finger ominously at his sister once more time. "Go set down somewhere"

Walking away to do just that Natalie still rolled her eyes.

Tiffany began with turning the body fully on its back. Getting one more look at Money Jay he muttered, "Dag Girl', how many bullets did you put into this man?" To which she just grinned.

"I told you he was trying to kill me, so I had to kill him first." Natalie folded her arms tightly together.

Tip turned his head, took a deep breath, then exhaled while grinding his teeth. He looked back over at Natalie to ask her for help, even though it was going to kill him by the end. "If you kindly don't mind, sis, can you please help me put this body into that duffel bag?" He looked as if he wanted to die.

Still with the grin on her face, "Wow, you want my help? I thought you didn't need my help, big brother Tiffany," she giggled at Tip as if she was trying to be funny, "I thought you told me to go and sit down somewhere. She got up and walked over to tap him on his back lightly with her hand. Then she whispered into his ear, "I think you got all this by your self, little bro."

Tip sneered at Natalie. Increasingly on this day he wanted to strangle her. "Look, I don't have to be here. You still don't get it; I can leave this body right here. It doesn't matter to me. It's your call. What are you going to do Natalie?" Tip looked at her up and down. Natalie stepped back and looked at her brother in a conflicted way, her smile slowly leaving her face.

"What the hell do you mean? You're going to leave this dead body? The hell you are!" She demanded shaking her head and pointing her finger back and forth between him and Jay.

Tip walked over close to Natalie with a smile on his face from here to California. "Now, that I have your attention Ms. Natalie James." His eyes so big they looked like fifty-cent pieces.

Natalie took a deep breath as she looked up at Tip. "OKay, I'll help you, but you have to promise me that you're going to put this body in your car plain and simple as that."

"Girl, you have really lost your damn mind. I'm not putting this nasty ass body in my car. Look at him, he looks like he has been dead for months. Besides this is your evidence, not mine." Tip took his arms and folded them across one another.

Natalie looked at her brother as if she wanted to slap him silly. "OKay, tell me one thing. Since he can't go into your car, then how the hell are we going to get this body out of the house? ...and into that little ass duffel bag, for that fact... since you know everything."

Tip looked back down at Money Jay's dead body, then back up at Natalie. "Well little sis, this is the part where you're going to be learning a few tricks."

Natalie stepped back as she put her hands on her hips. "What the heck are you talking about? And what darn tricks that I'm supposed to be learning." She smiled as she looked at her brother, with her hands still on her hips. "I haven't the slightest idea what you're talking about, OKay Tip, no freaking idea. What the heck are you about to do, enlighten me?" Natalie took her arms and folded them again – all attitude again.

"We are going to chop this body up, and put him into this black, pretty duffel bag you have here."

Before she could again admonish him for his crazy her phone rang. "Who in the hell could be calling me this time of the night?"

"Maybe it could be one of your lovers that you can't seem to get rid of."

"Yeah right, like I really got one of those." She looked back down at her phone. She was surprised when Jerry Cole's number came across it. "Oh shit, Tip, I can't answer this call right now."

"Why can't you answer the phone? Is it someone you are not expecting to call?"

However Natalie looked as if she had seen a ghost. Tip stopped fumbling with the duffel bag as he got up and walked a little closer to Natalie. "OKay Nat, apparently you want to tell me why you can't answer the phone."

Natalie took a deep breath, looked Tip deep in the eyes, grabbed Tip by the hand and replied, "OKay Tiffany, what I'm going to tell you; I don't want you to get upset with me."

Tip snatched his hand away from Natalie's as if she really had lost it this time. "OKay, are you going to tell me what the hell is going on, and who was that on the phone?"

"Well, that was a guy that I met in the park the other day..."

Tip yelled out, "Will you just get to the damn pointed?!"

Natalie jumped back "OKay, I am... If you just give me a moment."

Tip, again shaking his head, was well into losing his patience with her.

"Natalie, I am going to ask you this one last time; Who the hell was that on the phone?"

She knew that she had to tell Tiffany James something quickly. She took one foot and put it behind the other. "Well little brother, that was the police," looking at him as if she had lots more information where that had come from. Natalie held her hands out and waved them in the air, "... he is a very good friend of mine and I know we can trust him, OKay."

He really wanted to strangle her now. Instead he stared at Natalie with his mouth open half way. "What the hell do you mean that was the police and he is a very good friend of yours? Not only did you fail to mention that he was a cop, Natalie, you told the cops about what had happened in your apartment. You idiot! And again, why would you call the police, Natalie? Of all people in the world, you just had to call the cops. Do you know what that makes you look like? A Damn fool!" All Natalie could do was looked back over at Tip.

Natalie looked down at the floor. As she looked back up, big crocodile tears in her eyes, she took a deep breath in and wiped her face with both of her hands. "You really think if I knew he was a cop from the dam jump I would be talking to him? Crazy! I had no idea that he was a cop," Natalie stepped over the body to walk back over to the fireplace, "and besides ...right about now, I have no time to explain how I met or how I know this man, OKay. And another thing... we have to hurry up and get this body out of my apartment, before it starts to stink up the place." Natalie stood straight looking over at Tip, as if she's done playing with him this go around. Natalie took her finger and pointed right at Tiffany as if she was his mother. "Look after we are done with this body and dump it somewhere, in the river or woods, I really don't give a damn right about now. All I care about is getting this dead body out of here, and finding that damn Ted Rogers so he can tell us where the hell our little sister is."

Tip walked away shaking his head.

Chapter 12

As Natalie and Tip continued to move the body of Money Jay off the floor Natalie's phone began to ring yet again. She looked at Tip, Tip looked at her – his nostrils flared, his anger at her unabated.

"OKay, this is strange, why on earth is my phone ringing?"

Tip put his hands on his hips and rolled his eyes. "All I know is that it better not be who I think it is or I'm walking right out of that door." Tip looked at Natalie as she glanced down at the phone – he knew well who could be on the other end of the phone.

Natalie let it ring, over and over again. Tip made a face at Natalie that said he was getting tired of her phone ringing back to back. "Why aren't you going to answer it, or you're just going to let it ring? For crying out loud, answer it, will you?"

Natalie took a deep breath in as she looked back down at her phone again, "OKay! Damn, since you want to know so badly, who is on my phone... Here! Why don't you answer it then?" Tip glared straight at Natalie, then he smiled from ear to ear.

Tip reached for Natalie's Phone while still looking at her with a grin. "I really don't think you want me to do that, now do you, Natalie?"

Suddenly Natalie realized that she had Ted Rogers's number locked in her phone; She snatched her phone back from her brother so quickly that one would have thought it was the cops on the other end of the phone. "You know what? Why don't I just go ahead and answer this call?" Natalie's eyes brightened as if a twinkling little star was in them. Clearly she was up to no good. She turned her head away from Tip. "It could be my man calling me... you know?"

"No, I don't know, and when suddenly do you have a man?" Natalie looked back over at Tip still holding the phone up against her face. As she turned her head and stuck out her tongue.

"Whatever! I have a man, thank you very much." Natalie turned her head quickly back away and rolled her eyes. Suddenly Natalie hit the end button with a finger. "Look, why don't we just go ahead, and do what we have to do so we can get this over with? No more distraction from now on, OKay? Let's focus on getting this body out of here."

Tip turned looked back at Natalie and smiled ss if he had won the Mega Million lottery. "I thought you would never ask." Natalie and Tip began to struggle, trying to put Money Jay's dead body into one of Natalie's expensive name-brand bags that she called The Pink Luscious tote. The more they struggled with the dead weight the more Natalie felt like she was getting worn out. Natalie fell to her knees as if she had been working a nine to five hard-labor job. This prompted Tip to shake his head at Natalie yet again. He knew from the jump that she was going to be no help to him at all.

Tip was getting so out of breath, that he could barely say, "OKay! Natalie, will you stop playing? Help me with this damn body. Hell! He looks like he was part of some grizzly bear family. What did you feed him before you killed him?

Natalie stopped tugging yet again, as she looked back over at him sideways. "What the hell do you think I'm over here trying to do Mr. I-got-it? Don't start with me, Tiffany McKinley James."

Tip dropped Money Jay's upper body on the floor to frown again at Natalie. "Well Damn, Nat, why don't you just go ahead and tell the whole damn world my government name?"

Natalie, little grin on her face and her eyes squinched a little hard, faced him. With a fearless look, as if she was ready to kill again, she felt like she could slap the cowboy shit out of him. "Look, boy, ain't no one in Bonneville, Virginia don't know who the hell you are," then, with gritted voice because she was holding onto the bottoms of Money Jay's bloody feet, "Tip... stop playing with me, and help me move this ugly-tail body. Now come on... shit I'm tired."

When they finally got the body into the tote bag Natalie and Tip began to drag the whole kit and caboodle towards the front door. When they arrived at the door Natalie and Tip leaned their bodies and heads up against it, then both slid down the white wooden surface as if their own bodies weighed a ton each. Suddenly a knock happened on the front door three times.

Tip turned and looked at Natalie who looked back without the slightest idea who could be knocking at her door, nor why.

"Are you expecting any company? Please, Natalie, tell me you're not. I have to hope you didn't ask some to come over at a time like this."

Natalie got up off the floor, stood on her tiptoes to look out through the peep hole and came back shocked to see who was standing in front of her door. She started working through her memory trying to find out how the person knew where she stays. Natalie looked back down at her brother Tip. Natalie realized that they still had a dead man chopped up in a bag so she panicked, and she walked back and forth with her fingers in her mouth. Natalie started talking to herself aloud, "Oh my god. This can't be happening. Not now, shoot. Why is she here? What does she want? Why does this always have to happen to me? And how the hell did she know I live here, I never told her?"

Tip grabbed Natalie by both of her arms and centered her to face him. "OKay, stop! Look at me. Do you know who that person is at your front door?" Natalie looked up at Tip as if she had seen a ghost. She nodded her head to say yes. This time she put both hands full of fingers in her mouth, chewing off all the nail polish – what she had left. Tip stepped back from Natalie scowling clearly starting to get mad all over again. "OKay then, who the hell is at the front door?" Natalie took in a deep breath, cast an unusual look as if she really didn't want to tell him who the person was and bit down on her bottom lip. At this point Tip was really about to lose his patience with Natalie whom walked away hoping that he couldn't see right through her. Who was Natalie kidding, this was her brother Tip – he knew any and everything about Natalie Michelle James. Well if Natalie would try to tell Tiffany a lie, he would definitely know that she was up to no good. Tip had walked over toward the sofa where Natalie was sitting, looking as if she was scared for her life.

Tip lowered down on his knees. "Are you going to tell me what the heck is going on with you, and who is at your front door?"

All Natalie did was look up at Tip, then back down at the floor. Suddenly a voice shouted through the door, "Hey, Girl! Natalie, come on now, I know you home I see your car in the driveway." Tip's confusion grew. The voice on the other side yelled on through the door, "OKay Natalie, I know you're in there. Why don't you just open up for me. They just kept right on banging on the door over and over. By this time Tip had really lost his patience.

Tip simply looked down at Natalie. "Well, Natalie, aren't you going to open the door?"

Natalie was still sitting there as frozen as she could be until she forced herself to get up off the sofa and walk toward the front door. Natalie took a second look, as she looked back down at the black duffel bag that held Money Jay's bloody dead body in. She took in one last deep breath, turned and looked down at her feet – she noticed how stiff they felt felt a sickness rise in her stomach. She held and rubbed it because she felt like she wanted to throw up. Natalie opened up the door and in poured Amy Bullock, her best friend. Amy was known as a woman sniper. Although Natalie and Amy were known as the two badass sniper women that Ted Rogers only has on his payroll, right now she couldn't believe what she was seeing. Natalie was still trying to figure out what Amy Bullock is doing at her front door. Could it be that Mr. Ted Rogers sent her along to kill her for his $50,000? 'Hell, for that type of money I would go out and kill myselft,' she mused. Natalie stepped back from the front door to let Amy in further. She studied Amy in a weird way – it was unusual for Natalie to see one of her partners standing in her front doorway. Hell, not just her partner in crime, but her best friend as well.

"OKay Amy, What the hell are you doing coming to my apartment unannounced?" All Amy Bullock did was tilted her head to one side as she smiled.

Chapter 13

Amy Bullock checked out Natalie with a pair of hazel tinted eyes, under a Halle Berry hair cut. She laughed, "OKay Girl, you need to not play with me. You know exactly why I'm here."

Natalie cut her eyes and wobbled her head to look back at Amy. "Excuse you, what the hell you say to me? And another thing, why are you in my damn house? How the hell did you find me?"

Amy stepped back to take a second look at Natalie as if Natalie was one of her girlfriends she'd had the night before. "You do know we have a mission to go and do for the head boss, right?" Amy stepped now fully inside Natalie's apartment as if it was her own. Amy Bullock loved to make herself look like she's the hardest person in Bonneville, Va. However, everyone knew that when it comes down to handling business, or even being the toughest person in the gangster world, Natalie James was the girl whom everyone would call. Hell, Even Ted Rogers even knew that one. Natalie could get the job done without even getting her hands dirty. Even though she stole all of Ted Rogers's money, Natalie was still one of his mean sniper hit women.

Suddenly Natalie looked at Amy as if she wanted to take Amy Bullock by her head and sling her across the living room. She turned around and closed the front door behind Amy and started staring Amy up and down. She knew she was going to have a hell of a fight on her hands when it comes to Amy Bullock but she already knew she can beat her best game. This girl doesn't like to lose any competition – especially competition involving Natalie James. "OKay Amy, I am going to ask you this shit one time and one time only; What the hell are you doing here in my apartment, and who the hell told you where I lived?" Natalie had forgotten all about her brother Tip, even standing right next to Amy.

Tip walked a little closer to standing next to Natalie. Getting fed up with the hold shenanigans thing, Tip cut his eyes from Amy then back over at Natalie.

Amy then noticed the fresh blood stains on the white carpet. She then looked back up and over to where Natalie and Tip were standing. Next stood out the bloody duffel bag through the corner of her eye. All Amy did for now was just smile. She walked around in a circle over and over again to stop in the middle of the floor, then slowly reached behind her back with one hand. Amy leaned her head from one side to the other to crack her neck, followed by her knuckles, all the while pushing her chest out as if she were King Kong's wife. "Well I'm here because... I want us to go do some more business together, if that's OKay with you Natalie." Amy returned thekir gazes with a smirk.

Natalie turned her head and looked up at Tip, then she looked back over at Amy once again. She wore the expression of a pit bull dog. "What damn business? We never had any or never will have any business together, Amy. I thought you said we had to do some business for the boss man." Her next glance at Tip gave him the signal that something wasn't right.

Natalie had walked a little closer to where Amy Bullock was standing while snaking one hand up behind her back to reach slowly for her gun. The other hand remained in front of her tapping her leg over and over. Amy looked over at Tip then back at Natalie. With a lovely smiled upon her face, as if she didn't give a rat's ass how Natalie felt about her being there. Amy's only mission was to come and take down Natalie James if it could possibly be done. She saw Natalie began to slide her hand behind her back, already knew what type of girl Natalie could be, suspected that there was going to be some bloodshed. 'Either I kill her first or she's going to kill me. Hell, there was no chance of either one of us walking up out of here alive.' Even if she tried to pull her gun out first, Amy knew that there was no way in hell that she could beat Natalie James in a gunfight. She moved to back up with her hands up in the air, but Tip had quietly walked to get behind Amy. Suddenly Amy looked, outside the corner of her eye again. The more Tip would ease his way over behind Amy Bullock the more alert she had to become to the possibility of a fight with either or both.

Natalie still has her hand behind her back tapping on her gun. Her fingers reached the trigger, while she still looked straight at Amy as if she were the devil herself. Natalie slowly began to walk a little closer to Amy. Actually, she Natalie had been waiting for this fight between Amy and herself for a very long time. IN their world that seemed to happen a lot, especially if you knew the person very well.

"OKay, Amy Bullock I have no idea why or what you want, so you better tell me really why are you here before I blow your head off."

Amy raised one eyebrow and laughed, "You think I'm supposed to be afraid of you, and you're," pointing at Tip, "supposed to be a bodyguard that's behind me... Natalie James, y'all better think again, kiddos."

Natalie leaned her head back and also laughed as hard as she could. "I don't need my brother to be my bodyguard, Miss. Bullock. You keep forgetting that I am my own person. So you see, Miss Bullock, ..." but before Natalie could finish her sentence Amy cut her off.

"Cut the bull crap, Natalie James. You and I know damn well why I am here. So tell you little wolf dog over here to go and sit the hell down somewhere before he catches one of these bullets!"

Tip frowned looking at Natalie – he couldn't believe that this heifer called him that. As he stepped back away from Amy, Tip began slowly pulling his gun out from behind his back. Amy quickly pulled her gun, and she pointed it right at Tiffany's head even before he could take that step back. "Now I told you don't play with me Natalie, I alright know that you killed one of your partners."

Natalie looked at Amy in a weird way. She had no idea what Amy was talking about. Amy gestured with the gun at Tip's and Natalie's faces to indicate that she wanted them to move out of her way. She herself slowly backed away, but edged a little closer to the black duffel bag. Keeping the gun trained on them Amy bent down slowly – she zipped open the bloody duffel bag . Amy's eyes opened wide, surprised as if she had never seen a dead body before. She then stood up as if she was in shock from what she had just seen.

"What the hell did y'all do, Natalie?" The more Amy Bullock looked down at the bloody duffel bag, the more nervous she got. "OKay Natalie, again, and whatever the hell your name is, can you please tell me what the hell is going on here? Why is our business partner in a duffel bag cut all the hell all up? Amy still pointed the gun at the both of them, while Natalie laughed.

"You really don't want me to answer that, now do you Miss Bullock? Now, I asked you earlier why you were here, and you refused to answer my questions..." Natalie moved to slowly close the distance toward Amy. She looked at Amy as if she was going to be next.

Chapter 14

As Natalie drew closer to Amy she tried to slide closer to the front door. "Ah, I really don't think you hear me, Miss Bullock."

Amy took in a deep breath and swallowed hard. "I heard you dammit, but apparently you didn't hear what I said so, therefore, I really don't care what you're asking."

A knock came at the front door. All three individuals looked at one another, and everything fell silent. Amy, still waving her gun, whispered, "Don't nobody move or you will get a bullet." However, as Amy turned around to see who was knocking at the door, Tip ran up behind her and wrapped his arm around her neck. Amy and Tip struggled for the gun. "Get the hell off of me you little turd."

The knock at the front door kept on getting louder. "Hello, Natatlie, are you in there?"

Natalie spat out as quietly as should yell, "Get the gun, Tiffany, get the gun." Amy and Tip struggled over it hard enough that they wound up rolling around on the floor. The gun dropped out of Amy's hand, and Natalie looked over. Impatiently she yelled, "Would you get the damn gun, man, and stop playing around!"

Tip had stopped struggling and looked up as if he wanted to knock Natalie's head off of her shoulders. Tip had to pin Amy down with his right leg and added the other leg on her arms. As if he was trying to put his best wrestling moves on her. "OKay, what the hell do you think I'm over here trying to do, play mud fights or something?! How about you get over here and give me a little hand. This so-called friend lof yours is not a lightweight!" Natalie ran over to where Tip and Amy were tussling, but by the time she got over there they both were tied up into a giant pretzel. "Umh, a little help here."

Natalie bent down so she could try to pull both of them apart, but suddenly the doorbell rang. Natalie looked over at the front door, then back down at Tip and Amy another time. She pointed her finger at Amy's face. "You better not say one word or, so help me, I will put you over there in that black duffel bag! You got me? Don't play with me Amy Bullock!" She looked as if she really didn't care at all what Natalie James was babbling about. All Amy could hope was that whomever was at the front door would notice the noise that they all were making. Natalie straightened up and walked over by the door. As she turned around and looked back over at her brother and Amy for the second time Natalie took a deep breath. "OKay Nat. You got this, just ask who is at the front door, and if it's nobody you know, then you don't let them in – plain and simple." Natalie eased open the front door, and she slowly peeked her head out of it.

Natalie couldn't believe who was standing in her doorway. She had to switch modes to play the ruckus off with a big smile from ear to ear as if everything was peaches and cream. "Well hey, Mr. Lincoln. What can I do for you?"

Mr. Terry Lincoln was a middle aged man, and typically all he would do is sit on his porch and stare at everything that walked by. "Hey, young lady," Terry turned around and faced Natalie with his old shaggy smile, "I just want to come over and see if you need anything." Normally, though, Mr. Lincoln wouldn't even try to lend a hand for anything if he could help it unless it was only about him.

Natalie looked back over at Tip and Amy. She turned back to Mr. Lincoln, "No, no, I think I'm OKay for right now." Natalie still had the fake smile upon her face, as if she wished that he would leave from in front of her door. She turned and closed the front door to hurry back to what she was doing.

"Now, where was I? Oh yeah, getting ready to kill you if you don't tell me why you are here."

Amy tried to get up off the floor. "Uhhh, excuse me, can you please get your muscular legs off of my legs and arms? Thank you Sir."

Tip chuckled "Let's not talk about muscles, woman you got me beat."

Amy tried again, "Will you get the hell off of me, please! You are hurting me, dammit!"

Natalie poked her lips upward. "Will you two cut it out before I shoot both of you. You both are starting to get on my last nerve." So Tip and Amy both got up off of the floor. "OKay so, now that I have your undivided attention; we are going to take a ride back to the warehouse, and you're going to tell me what you and Mr. Ted Rogers have got going on."

Amy turned and looked at Natalie with a beautiful smile that belied that she wasn't going to tell Natalie James anything. "What mades you think that, I'm going to tell you or your paw patrol over here anything I know." Amy Bullock was still looking at Natalie with that grin on her face.

"OKay, let's go before I put all nine rounds in your head because, bitch, before you walk out that door you're going to tell me; what is the Plan with you and Mr. Rogers?"

Tip looked at Natalie. "OKay, well what are we going to do with this bag?"

Natalie turned her head slowly and looked back over at Tip, "We are going to get rid of it. Just like we are going to get rid of her if she doesn't let me in on what's the 411." Natalie tapped her finger on her bottom lip, then she turned around and pointed the gun straight at Amy's head. "You know what? I'm just sick of this crap!"

Natalie pulled the trigger and shot Amy Bullock nine times.

Tip stepped back, looking at Natalie as if she had lost her ever loving mind. "What the hell is wrong with you? You do know she was our lead to tell us where our baby sister is!" Natalie turned round and looked at Tiffany as if he was the one that had lost his mind.

"She wasn't going to tell us anything. That's why her ass had to die. Know that if you want to be next just say the word, and I'll be happy enough and do you it, big brother. I'm not in the mood for any of your mess either."

Tip leaned his posture back and smiled. "I really don't think you want to do that, Miss James," as he went to walk away he stopped at the front door, and turned to looked back at Natalie, "if I was you? I would check out my resume. Matter of fact, here." Tip bent down to pick up Amy Bullock's bloody phone and brought it over to Natalie. "While you're at it, Google me up. That should tell you all about me. Stop playing with me girl. Now you know how I get down, so let's get these two bodies out of this so-called condo and see if we can still find that ugly Ted Rogers, your so-call boss." Natalie looked back over at the dead bodies while frowning up her face.

They both grabbed the dead bodies out of the house. Mr. Lincoln happened to be sitting on his porch. "Hey there, my neighbor! What you got here?" Natalie stopped in the middle of the driveway to look at Mr. Lincoln as if she had no idea what he was talking about. "Hey, I can help you with that.

Natalie snatched the black, bloody duffel bag away. "No!, I got it, thank you. I got it from here."

Tip was on his way out with Amy Bullock over his shoulder until he saw Mr. Lincoln standing there trying to help Natalie with the duffel bag. "Uh, Nat, we really have to get a move on. You know our big sister isn't feeling very well...?"

Mr. Lincoln still insisted upon trying to help. "Hey, son, let me give you a hand with her."

Tip looked over at Natalie then back at Mr. Lincoln. "No Sr.! I am good, I got it. Thank you for your wonderful, kind help, but we got it from here." Tip's eyes widened as Natalie threw the duffel bag into the trunk of the car. Next he lay Amy down on the back seat, covered with blood, with one bullet hole as big as a fifty cent piece right in the middle of her head.

Natalie and Tip drove around for at least an hour when one of them finally broke the silence. "Look, we need to find a spot to dump these bodies before someone notices that we keep riding in the same places."

Natalie turned her head slightly toward Tip. "OKay, where the heck am I going to dump them at? They sure can't stay in my car all night."

Tip looked back over at Natalie, With a light grin on his face. "Well we can dump them into the Chesapeake Bay. I am quite sure, no one is going to find them out there."

As they both began to look at one another sideways, Tiffany and Natalie smiled at one another. Natalie's phone rang. "Oh my God! What is it now? I am so sick of this damn phone ringing."

Tip turned and looked back over at Natalie. "Well, you are always calling yourself the most popular girl in Bonneville."

Natalie squinched her eyes and turned her head away. "Well Hell, I am, and don't forget – the baddest bitch that ever walked in Bonneville, too." Tiffany just leaned his head away as he shook it. She answered her phone, "Yes, hello? Who is this?" Natalie Started to look around inside the car as if the person could be next to her. "I said who is this? Hello? Can you hear me?" All Natalie heard on the other end of the phone was silence. She pulled over on the side of the road and looked over at Tip.

"What the hell was that all about?" Tiffany was still looking at her in a weird way, as if he was just as confused as she was. "Well, who the heck was on the phone?"

Natalie looked back over at Tip for a second time. "I don't know. They didn't say anything, but I got a pretty good idea on who it could be."

Tip looked even more confused. "OKay, then who?" He threw his hands up. "I know one thing: it had better not be that damn Ted Rogers that was on the phone."

All Natalie did was turn her head and drove off.

Chapter 15

They turned back to the house where Natalie pulled the car into the driveway. What the hell is he doing here now? As she and her brother got out of the car Natalie was really starting to look confused. Jerry Cole was standing right in front of her doorstep. "Hey, what are you doing here? I didn't know you were coming over." Jerry, just smiled.

"Well, I tried to call your phone, but you didn't answer, so I thought I would drop by. So here I am." While Natalie turned and looked back at Tip with surprise. Jerry still looked at Natalie like maybe he wanted to throw her down and start making out with her. "Well how about we go inside for a little chit-chat?"

Natalie took a deep breath in, "Hmm; Well, I don't think that would be a good idea. You see, I haven't had time to clean up, and my house is just a mess."

Tip leaned his head back to eye her, as if she was crazy. Of course he already knew why her house was a total disaster.

Jerry continued trying to convince Natalie to change her mind, "I don't mind a little mess here and there. Heck, if you want me to I'll help you clean up." Natalie's eyes opened wide as fifty cent pieces. She turned and looked back over at her brother for a third time.

Tip leaned his head back to think to himself, 'If she thinks that I'm going to leave her here with this man that I don't know – she has another thing coming.' Tip folded his arms. And leaned a bit to one side, as if he was trying to tell her, 'I'll wait...' while also studying both of them up and down.

Jerry turned from looking at Natalie to Tiffany James. "Well, I see you have a lot going on right now. So I'll just come back another time."

Tip whispered under his breath, "Yeah! You better get ready to go," meant just for himself.

Jerry looked back at Natalie and smiled and waved 'goodbye.' as he was getting into his car.

Tip looked back over at Natalie, "What the hell was that all about?"

Natalie frowned, still waving goodbye to Jerry, "I don't know, but I'm damn sure going to find out. But in the meanwhile," Natalie turned and looked at Tip in a helpless way, "Uhm, bro, can you help me get that mess up that we left in my living room."

Tip shook his head and laughed, "Girl!, What in the world would you do without me if I wasn't around?" All Natalie could do was look back at Tip and laugh along with him. As they both went back into the house Natalie heard some weird sounds.

Natalie turned and looked back over at Tip once again. "Did you hear that?"

Tip reached for his gun. "I thought you said there was no one else here."

Natalie frowned even more deeply. "There isn't no one else here." The noise got a little louder.

Natalie and Tip slowly walked toward the kitchen. As they edged closer they were surprised when they found out who it was in the Kitchen. "Well, well I just know that your scrawny little ass is not in my kitchen," Natalie folded her arms across her chest wearing an angered-woman face. "What the hell are you doing coming out of my my laundry room, Ted Rogers?"

Tip kept his gun pointed right at Ted Rogers' back. "OKay, Natalie let me go ahead and take this fool out, because I don't think he is going to tell us where our baby sister is."

Natalie took out her gun and pointed it at Ted Rogers, too. "Oh, yes the hell he is, or I will pull my trigger. I'm not my brother, so don't play with me. Tell me where my sister is." Ted still had his hands up, and he slowly turned around to look at Natalie as if he was ready to die.

"I don't know, and I don't care where she is. All I know you better have my $50,000 or, like I said, your head will be on a meat platter."

Natalie leaned her head to one side at Ted's statement with a little grin. "You're sitting up here saying what you are going to do to me, and I'm the crazy bitch – with the gun in my hand. How are you still talking smack?" Natalie walked over a little closer to Ted and slaps him with the gun. "OKay for real, I'm damned tired of playing with you. Now, tell me where my kid sister is."

Ted was still looking at Natalie while laughing. "I'm not telling you anything, bitch!"

Natalie looked back over at Tip and then once again at Ted. "Oh yeah, you not, huh?" Natalie pointed the gun and shot Ted Rogers right in his left foot. "Now, the next one is going to be in your ass, if you don't stop playing with me boy!"

Ted Rogers fell to the floor. He looked back up at Natalie and wailed, "Bitch, you shot me! Are you crazy, or you have just lost your mind?"

Natalie bent down over Ted, "Yeah I am – crazy as hell... now, like I said, if you don't give me what I want, 'Bye bye, Ted Rogers,' you got that?"

All he could do was nod his head while holding on to his bloody foot. "OKay, OKay, I have her down at the waterside, but trust me, what you are going to see is not what you think."

Natalie straightened up and kept the gun pointed at Ted. "Well, I'll just have to take my chance now, won't I? As a matter of fact, you are going to take me straight to her, so get up off your tail and show me where she is."

Ted took in a deep breath and then exhaled a hot one out. "Hey man, why don't you tell your sister to ease up a little; She did just shoot me in the foot, you know?"

Tip leaned over to look at Ted's injury, but his face said he could care less if he was hurt or not. "Tell you the truth, I kinda like the way she is handling things. Now, like she said, get up before I end up putting a bullet in you myself."

Ted got off the floor slowly. "So that's how this is going to work... Both of y'all are going to gang up on me."

Natalie had begun to pace in a circle. "Look! I told you, before that I don't need my brother or anyone else to do my job! Especially includes you, of all people, Mr. Rogers! So now get up off the floor and show me where you got my sister – for the last time!"

A knock rapped at the front door. Natalie snap-turned and caught eyes with Tip. Then she looked back over at Ted, "So help me, if you scream I will put the bullet right in your head!" Natalie took her finger and put it across her lips. Then to Tip she whispered, "Maybe if we don't answer the door then whoever it is will leave."

Ted laughed again, "You really think it's that easy – they're just gonna go away. Look around, you two: you have me in here held up with a gunshot wound to the foot. And plus, y'all's cars are out in front."

Natalie advanced on Ted Rogers, "Didn't I just tell you to shut up? Don't say another word! Damn, your head is hella hard!"

Tip got Natalie's attention, "You do know he is right, Nat?"

"I beg your pardon! What did you say? Excuse me! Now you're on his side now? Well I'll be damn my own brother done switch up on me."

Tip backed up and looked at Natalie as if she really had lost her mind. "Now wait one damn minute, Natalie. You know dag well I will never take anyone else's side, except yours. You are my sister and I will kill for you Natalie. You know that. What do you want me to do, kill him? Is that what you are implying?"

Natalie turned her head to the wall and then back at Tip, "You know – that wouldn't be a bad idea." Natalie took her finger and tapped it on the bottom of her chin.

Tip fixed Natalie with a weird look, "You're sick, you know that?"

"Hey, I took my medicine this morning. Now back to you Mr. Rogers; Don't Play with me. I'm going to go and see who is at my front door, and you'd better not made one sound. You got it?" The doorbell rang and kept ringing. "Oh my God, really do you have to keep ringing my doorbell like you have lost your mind?" As Natalie opened the door she was not surprised at who appeared on the other side, "Oh it's you. That figures... it's my nosy neighbor, Mr. Terry Lincoln. What is it that I can do for you now, Mr. Lincoln?" The man was standing in Natalie's doorway wearing a big smile on his face until he heard her nasty remark.

"Well dag, I just came over to see how you were doing and if you and the gentleman that you were with needed anything..."

Natalie held her stomach as she laughed, then replied, "No you didn't, Mr. Lincoln, you came over here to see what was going on in my damn house with your nosy-old ass. Now get away from my door, before I do something to you that we both are all going to regret!" Natalie turned back around and slammed the front door in Mr. Lincoln's face.

Chapter 16

"Ahhh! He got on my last nerves!" Natalie balled both her fists up tightly, ready to punch someone. "OKay, this shouldn't take long, after he tells me what I need to know." As Natalie walked back into the kitchen, however, she found her brother Tip and Ted Rogers were fighting over Tip's gun. She took the gun out from behind her back once again and fired it into the air twice. "What the hell is going on here?! Have you two lost your minds? I go to the front door and come back. And you two are sitting up here acting like two cave animals!" Tip and Ted hustled to get off the floor. "Now, since I have your attention, let's get back to the basics shall we?" They both straightened up, yet sneered at Natalie as if she smelled like a zoo animal. "OKay, why in the hell are you two nut cakes looking at me?"

"Look, it doesn't matter how long you try to keep me here, or even bash my head in, I'm still not going to tell you where your sister is."

Natalie walked over toward where Ted Rogers was standing. "Oh! So we are still on that again, right? I'll tell you what: how about I just go outside and set your new Lincoln LX Town Car on fire? What do you think, Tip, do you think we need that?"

Ted's eyes widened. "OKay! Damn, I'll show you where she is. Just don't touch my baby outside."

Natalie turned around and pointed her finger to the front room door. "What... that nice white and gold car with the chrome wheels on them? Naw, you can't be talking about that nice-ass car outside! If you are... 'BABY', heh, she ain't nice no more – not after Miss Natalie James got through with her!" Ted turned and looked back at Natalie as if he wanted to kill her, yet now he needs her help. "So how about we get into that burnt car of yours?"

Ted hung his head and walked toward the front door with tears in his eyes, head down as if he had just lost his best friend.

Natalie looked back at Tip, then burst out in loud laughter at Ted Rogers, "Lordy, you should have seen your face when I said your car was in flames!" Natalie kept right on laughing, as if a comedian had told the joke in her living room. Tip looked back over at Natalie, then at Ted Rogers and started to laugh, also.

"Oh! So you both think this shit is funny, right? See how funny it is when you can't find your sister Jessica!" The more they laughed the angrier Ted became. "Haha! You two really think that was funny, don't you?!"

Tip looked back over at Ted with tears coming from out of the sides of his eyes from laughing so hard. Then Tip realized what Ted Rogers had said about finding his little sister. Tip suddenly stopped laughing and looked back up, cutting his eyes in Ted's direction. "What the hell do you mean if we can't find our little sister Jessica? Man don't you... I would... blow your head all over these nice white walls."

Natalie jumped in between both gentlemen. "OKay, first of all," as she turned and looked back at Ted, "you will tell us where my sister is. And far as you go Mr. Tip, you will not be painting no-one's head onto my shiny, white walls. Are you crazy?" Tip still had the gun pointed directly right at Ted Rogers' face as if to say 'one move and you're dead.'

Natalie turned around to say something to her brother Tip; To her shock she found that she, too, was looking down a gun barrel. "Ahh, I think you need to back the hell up, Mr. James, before I put a bullet in the both of you. Now... if you don't mind, let's go and find my sister, Ted... before your brains be scattered all over my carpet." As they headed out the door, Natalie turned back and looked at Ted Rogers again. "And for the record don't think you getting out of this easily because you're taking me to find her. Don't get it twisted

I still want you dead." However, Ted Rogers turned his head back and looked at Natalie to smile as if he was already dead to her.

On their way out Natalie noticed that Mr. Lincoln was standing by his car. 'Dammit! Now, how are we going to get to my car when we have Mr. Nosy box outside.'

Ted looked at the both of them and laughed, "Oh, this here should be interesting..."

Tip made a face at Ted, while shoving him outside the condo door. "Will you just shut the hell up and get into the car."

Mr. Lincoln did look over at Natalie, but then he squinted his eyes, turned and walked back into his house. Natalie thought it was kind of strange, the way Mr. Lincoln had just turned and walked back into the house without nagging or even trying to offer his help. Natalie scrunched her face up a little, as she turned and looked back at her brother Tip.

"Did you see that? He didn't even say a word, or even try to look over this way..."

Tip nodded his head. Although he couldn't even believe that Mr. Lincoln didn't say a word, either, both of them just shrugged at one another and continued to get into the car. "Well, let's not drink any spoiled milk. We still have a mission to get to before it gets too late."

Natalie was still bothered about Mr. Lincoln and how he was acting, but said, "Yeah, I guess you are right. Let's get a move on." Still she caught herself glancing back over at Mr. Lincoln's house, wondering what was going on with her nosy next door neighbor. She pointed Ted Rogers towards the back seat of her car, while squinting her eyes as if she wanted to slap him into next week.

"OKay, Mr. I-can-hold-a-secret, we are going back to your place to get some more cash and-"

Ted cut Natalie off, "And why do we need to go to my house to get some more cash?"

However, by the time Natalie went to reply, A loud, green 1965 Cadillac with dark tinted windows and gold and silver trim came speeding down the street at them.

Tip looked urgently at Natalie, "Do you know who they are?" Then snapped his head back over at the green car for the second look.

At the same time Mr. Lincoln walked back outside. Natalie looked even more confused.

"What the hell is going on here?" Tip asked, walking toward that car.

"I don't know and I'm really not trying to find out, either. So if I was you I would just get the car as fast as I can," but by the time Natalie went to jump back into her car the green Cadillac came rushing down the street blowing its horn. "OKay, what the hell was that all about?"

Ted jumped back out of Natalie's car, "Look! If you want me to tell you where your sister is then I suggest that you do what I want... then you will see your little sister."

Tip and Natalie turned and looked at one another and laughed. "You have got to be out of your rabid-assed mind if you think that I'm going to made a deal with the devil himself. You have another think coming." Natalie walked slowly toward Ted Rogers. She looked up at him with fire in her eyes. In her low, soft voice, "Mr. Rogers, you keep right on forgetting *That I Am The Devil*. Now get your tall-legged ass into the damn car before I shoot both of them off."

Later on that night as they pulled up at Ted Rogers' house Natalie slowly turned back and looked over at Ted. "I'm telling you now; don't play with me. If my sister is not in this house, I will kill you myself."

Ted Rogers leaned his head back against the head rest with a big smile upon his face. "If you kill me how on earth are you going to find your beloved sister Jessica James?" Natalie went to grip Ted by his shirt front, but Tip grabbed Natalie by her arm.

"If you kill him, then we will never find our sister. So please, chill out for right now." Natalie slowly took her hand away from Ted Rogers' shirt. As soon as Natalie had turned her head Tip reached across the back seat. "OKay, now this is me you're dealing with. I'm not my sister nor do I give a rat's ass about how you feel. You will walk your little, happy-go-lucky ass into that house and hand my baby sister over to me. You got that?"

Ted Rogers coolly looked at Tip with a light grin on his face, "...And if I don't? You're going to kill me no matter what. So how about you go right on and just do it, because I'm not telling you a damn thing."

Natalie opened up the back set of the car, "OKay, that's it! I'm tired of your B.S. You can laugh all you want to Ted Rogers, but you need to know I'm not playing around with you. Don't forget I used to work for you." Ted's smile slowly left his face. "Now that I have your full attention. How about we walk into that nice, big house of yours and you give me what I want.

As they walked up toward the house one of Ted's bodyguards opened the front door. "Wait, what the hell is going on here, Natalie? Uh, why do you have our boss at gun point?" Natalie leaned back, and cracked a smile. "Your Boss huh, well, Mr. Fisher, he has something, or shall I say some*one* that belongs to me."

He looked at Natalie as if she had completely lost her mind. "Are you insane? Have gone mad, girl? I wonder what the hell is wrong with you?

Tip came on the other side of Natalie. "How about you just shut the hell up, and move out of our way before you catch a bullet in your head?"

Micheal leaned, looking at Tip as if he had also lost his mind. "...And may I ask who the hell are you?" Almost everyone had a gun pointed at another.

Natalie and her brother Tiffany James had turned their backs, toward one another. "Maybe you need to ask your so-called boss, who I am..."

All Micheal did was stare as he held his gun on them. "Don't think for one second, I'm going to ease up off of you two. If you think that, then I know the both of you are crazy. And as for your concern Natalie James..."

Chapter 17

"...like I said, before you two clowns came barging in here like you own the place." Micheal Fisher turned and looked at Ted Rogers while still pointing his gun at Natalie and Tip.

"Yeah, I'm OKay, just these two fools want to know where their sister Jessica is." mentioned Ted.

Micheal laughed, "You two gotta be the dumbest people I have ever known."

Tip and Natalie kept their guns aimed directly at them, hoping that one of them would make a move. "Well, as far as we know you are holding my sister against her will. So if I was you, I would let her go – or we all are going to be, some dead *bitches* in here today. Now like I said, give me what I came for."

Micheal looked back at Ted Rogers, then over at Tip and Natalie. "Girl, please, you don't scare anybody in this damn house."

Natalie took a step back and glared at Micheal Fisher again, "Oh yeah? I don't huh?" She aimed lower and shot him in the leg. "So, do I scare your non-talking ass now? I told you, I'm not the one to be playing with."

Micheal dropped the gun out of his hands and fell to the ground. "*Bitch*... are you crazy?! You just shot me in my leg!" With blood dripping everywhere all Micheal Fisher could do now was hold his leg tightly.

Natalie could care less if he lived or died, all she was concerned about was bringing her little sister home safe. "Are you going to give me what I asked for, or do I have to finish off what I started?"

Micheal looked up at Natalie and starts to shook his head, "OKay Damn! I'll give you what you want, but on one condition," before Micheal could even finish his sentence Natalie's phone started ringing over and over again.

She answered it with, "Damn, what do you want?!"

The voice on the other end was very polite as they responded back to her, "I want you Ms. Natalie James." She couldn't believe what her ears and eyes were telling her. She dropped her phone out of her hand. Jerry Cole just walked out of Ted Rogers' kitchen with a big, happy smile on his face, as if he knew one day she was going to walk right into his trap. "I want you Miss Natalie. How hard it is for you to see that? Oh, and I want your toy friend you've got with you, too." Jerry was still looking at her smiling as though nothing had ever happened.

Natalie just still couldn't believe her eyes. "What the hell is going on here Jerry? For crying out loud, aren't you are a police officer?"

Jerry walked slowly over to Natalie. With his hand he moved Natalie's gun slowly out of his face. "Yeah, I am a cop, oh and a thief by night," his smile unwavering, "so you see, Miss James, I know all about your little sister, and your business with Ted Rogers; Which is nothing to me. That is just as long as I get my share of money. So, you see, if you want your sister back I suggest you start to cooperate, and do what I ask you to do, or there will be no little sister to be found. You got that? Now, first tell your partner over here to drop his weapon, and I suggest you drop yours, too, Miss James."

Natalie stepped back and realigned the gun with Jerry. "You must be crazy, thinking that I'm going to lower my gun and let you kill me first. Not a chance brother." As she looked back over at her brother Tiffany and nodded at him. "And your ass better not lower your gun either, Tip."

Tip laughed back to her, while keeping Jerry Cole in his sight. "Not on my lifetime sister, I'm not going to put a damn thing down. So if you want her you have to come through me."

Jerry turned back toward Natalie with a lean to his head and a light grin on his face. "Well, well, I see that you have your little fan club support." As he continued to laugh at Natalie and her brother Jerry was very sure of Natalie's next move. In fact the more he looked at her, the more he was starting to get a little scared himself. Jerry rubbed his face, hard then he walked over her way, he then grabbed Natalie by her throat.

"Let me go you ass bucket!" But the more Natalie tried to get away from Jerry the tighter he would hold on – then, in turn, the more Natalie would try and fight.

"There is no use, Miss James, you belong to me now." Before Jerry could even turn around, Tip had the gun stuck right at the back of Jerry's head.

"Now if I was you I would let my sister go, before your brains are scattered all over this damn floor. And as for you, Ted Rogers, You are lucky that I just don't go right ahead and kill you first. As a matter of fact..." then suddenly Tip pointed the gun and shot Ted Rogers again in the same leg.

"What the hell is wrong with you people?! You can't just go around and shoot people for no damn reason! You damn crazy-ass fool!"

Tiffany's arm snapped back over at Jerry, "Now that I have your attention, how about letting my sister go, or you will be next."

Jerry eased his hand from around Natalie's neck, and began to back up slowly with his hands up. Natalie rubbed her neck over and over again, as she looked back up at him. She still couldn't believe that man who had taken her out to dinner and promised to wine and dine her was with her enemy – the untrustworthy boss, Ted Rogers, who was plotting to kill her and her baby sister. What kind of man would want to hurt a young and beautiful woman? Surely her eyes were deceiving her.

"OKay, so how much is he paying you to kill me? Because if it's what I think it is, oh brother, I can triple that amount."
Jerry laughed, "Sweetheart, I don't want your money, I want you dead."

Natalie stepped in on Jerry Cole and suddenly hauled off and punched him dead in his face. Jerry stumbled from the hit.

"What the hell is wrong with you, girl? Are you crazy: hitting me like you have lost your damn mind." Jerry went to draw back and strike her back until he realized that her brother, Tip, still had the gun pointed at him. Natalie bent down on the floor to pick up her gun that she had dropped.

"I am getting very tired of playing games with you two meatheads. Oh yeah! I almost forgot about you sir," Natalie looked down at Micheal Fisher once again. She honestly had completely forgotten that he was there. At this point Micheal could barely move because he had gushed so much blood from his leg. He even looked like he was about to die, but Natalie didn't really seem to care if he could move or not, "OKay you, get up before I take away your other leg." She turned back to Jerry, "How about you take both of your dead dogs business partners down to the basement and tie them up?"

Jerry looked at Natalie with a madman's face, "Now why in the hell would I tie up, my boss and one of our business partners?"

Natalie laughed while holding on to her stomach, "What do you mean, 'My business partner'? Hell, he stopped being my business partner right after he kidnapped my little sister."

"... And what do you mean kidnapped?" Jerry stepped a little further away from Natalie, "Do you really want to know the whole damned truth about your so-called baby sister?"

Before Jerry could finish his conversation with Natalie, though, Ted Rogers butted in as he hollered out, "No, Jerry, don't... it's best that she doesn't know about her sister Jessica."

Natalie's brother looked even more confused. "Wait! What the hell does he mean it's best for her not to know?" Ted, Jerry and Micheal all began to look at one another as if they had a secret that wasn't supposed to be revealed. "I asked a question! What do you know about our sister Jerry?" Jerry turned as if to walk away with a slight grin on his face, but then Jessica was coming down the stairs, "If she has one scratch on her, or one piece of hair re –."

Jessica continued down the big white stairs and interrupted Tiffany, "Please go on, Jerry, and finish telling my two lovely siblings how I want them both dead... and help him off the floor and get him some medical attention before he bleeds all over my floor."

Natalie and Tip stayed looking confused. Tip even shook his head. Natalie walked in a circle around her sister Jessica to look her over.

"So you mean to tell me that your little dusty ass isn't hurt, or about to *die* or shall I say? NOT EVEN KIDNAPPED?! Do you know what your little red ass put me through?"

Tip's thoughts also cleared enough to declare, "Uh, excuse me, but I think she had me worried too."

Natalie looked back over at Tip with a frown. "Boy, this not about you right about now. I'm talking about her little scrawny ass." Natalie stopped going around her baby sister. "Why would you pull such a horrible scam like this, Jess. What have I ever done to you?"

Jessica laughed, "You don't get it, do you Nat? All those times when you really thought that you were working for the big man, Ted Rogers, over here you were really working for me; your pain-in-the-butt little sister."

Natalie took a deep breath in and exhaled a big sigh out. In Natalie's soft voice she uttered, "Girl, I'm about to kill you."

Natalie stepped toward her, but this time Tip grabbed Natalie and pulled her back. Jessica's eyes had gotten wide because she knew what Natalie was capable of, however the smile upon her face had not diminished.

"So do you think that I did all of this just for a show, my dear sweet sister, Natalie?"

Natalie yelled out, "*Bitch!* When I get my hands on you I'm going to tear your little, ugly head off your damn body! *Come here, you little--*"

Natalie went to reach for Jessica again, but by that time the latter had run behind Jerry, and Jessica began to yelled out, "Get her

Jerry, don't let her kill me! I'll pay you double to do that for me. Please!"

Tip, looked back over at Jessica, "What is wrong with you? This is your sister we are talking about here. So you're really going to kill your only sister, Jess, just so you can have some kind of total control?"

Jessica peaked her head from around Jerry, "You damn right, I'm going to kill her ass before she kills me. On second thought," Jessica walked from behind Jerry, "I just might kill your ass, too."

Tiffany stepped back and leaned his head to one side. "I know you've done lost your damn mind; talking about killing me. Girl, do you know what I will do to you?" Tiffany looked at Jessica as if she was going to die right then and there.

"Oh I'm not so much worried about you at all, big brother, but on the other hand," Jessica pointed her finger at Natalie, "this bitch right here I am worried about. So you see, Tip, there is no need for you to jump on Natalie's band wagon when," Jessica turned around in a circle holding her arms out, "you can have all of this right here."

Natalie's face held a frown. "You know what?" She ran toward her sister, Jessica again. "You really think I'm going to let you get away with this? Hell will freeze over before I'll let you do that, Missy!"

Suddenly Tip ran up behind Natalie and hit her over the head with his gun. Natalie promptly fell on the floor.

Jessica stood over her sister. "Well damn, what took you so long? She could have killed me, you jackass."

Tip looked at Jess and shook his head. "Yeah, but she didn't. So if I was you, I would go ahead and tie her crazy ass up. Oh, and take her gun and make sure she does not find it." Jessica poked her lips out at him. Tip walked over toward where Jess was standing. "You do know that when she wakes up I am a dead man thanks to you, right?"

Jessica turned and looked back over at Tip sideways. "Yeah, I do know she is going to kill you, but if I don't stop Natalie James now then we're all going to be dead around here."

Chapter 18

Later on that night Natalie awoke to find herself chained to the wall. "Oh, you bitches, when I get out of here I'm going to kill all of you!"

Tip noted to Jess, "Well, I think your big sister has come to."

Jessica turned back and looked with an eyebrow up. "Yeah, so what? I hear the little bitch. What you want me to do about it?"

Tip frowned. "What do I want you to do? I want you to fix this mess that you have created, Jess. That's what I want you to do."

Jessica huffed, "OKay, dag, I will go and check on the big ass baby down in the basement." As she went to walk toward the basement door Jessica stopped and looked back over at Tip. "Hey! Have you seen Amy and Money Jay anywhere around here lately? I wonder where they've been; it's not like them at all. Hey, if you see them can you please let them know that I'm looking for them? I really need them to do some work for me." Tip just looked at Jessica and walked away. As Jessica entered the basement where Natalie was chained she announced, "Look, you are making too much damn noise down here. Quiet it down before you wake up my neighbors."

Natalie looked up and laughed, "Your neighbors? Damn you and your neighbors. So help me, Jess, when I get from out of here I'm going to kill you. And tell your Watch dog Tiffany that's supposed to be our brother that he is next; I'm going to get his butt last."

Jessica walked over to where Natalie was chained up with a false aire of politeness. "Bitch, shut-up, 'cause you can't do nothing. So if where you, I would just be quiet and behave like you supposed to."

Natalie pulled the chain as she jumped at Jessica. "Oh, bitch you are so mine when I get loose from here. I'm going to--" But when Natalie tried to finish her sentence Jess cut her off.

"Yeah, Yeah, you are not going to do anything Nat. Come on, be for real, what possibly can you do, huh? I mean look at you. You are chained up to a wall. And besides, you look like hell, if you ask me."

Natalie turned her head and rolled her eyes. "So help me when I get out of here, I promise you, you're going to be the first to go. You really think this is funny don't you, little bitch? Mark my words I'm going to--"

Tip, walked into the basement. "Look, I know you got to be hungry, so here, why don't you just eat a little bit of this soup that I made for you?"

Natalie hung her head over as she grunted her discontent as if she already knew what he was up to, "You gotta be crazy, thinking that I'm going to eat that food!" Natalie looked sideways and laughed at him.

Tip looked down at her pityingly. "OKay Nat, look, no one is trying to kill you. I just want to made sure you have something on your stomach." When he bent down and tried to feed her the food Natalie reached up and knocked the bowl out of Tiffany's hand. Tip jumped up very quickly, "Are you crazy? Look, if you don't want to eat that's on you, but you will not be throwing food at me like I'm a damn animal."

Jessica burst out with a loud laugh, "You really think that she is going to eat from you Jackass? I think not." Natalie looked up a little weak and sickly. Tip stood up to pace.

"Please, Nat, eat for me. I promise I'm not trying to kill you OKay?" Jessica continued to laugh. "Will you shut the hell up? You ain't doing nothing but making things worse by laughing."

Jessica walked toward the basement door. "OKay, fine. Suit yourself, but I'm telling you that she is not going to eat." Jessica left out.

"OKay, it's just you and I now. So please, Natalie, eat for me."

She looked up at him once again suddenly, only this time she pretended as if she was going to eat the food; Natalie opened her mouth, and Tip reached and handed her the food, but when he bent down to feed her, the latter quickly dipped her body backward and scooted her waist upward to lift her legs up high. She successfully wrapped them around Tiffany's neck as tightly as she could get them. They both struggled around on the basement floor until a muffled crack sound came from Tip's neck. Natalie slowly, gently lay him down to the cold, hard floor, then she reached for the key to unlock herself.

Natalie got up off the floor, she then looked back down at her brother as he lay there dead from a broken neck. She wondered if she could do the same to her sister Jessica. Natalie pulled Tip's body into a corner. She looked around to find something to cover his body with – an old dirty sheet that she threw over him.

'OKay, there, that should do it. Now I have to do is find that no-good traitor sister of mine. When I do I'm going to do the exact same thing to her. Watch and see if I don't.' With the look in Natalie's eyes one could tell that revenge on her sister and her so-called boss man, Ted Rogers was her sole drive. She thought on, 'Oh Mr. Jerry Cole, don't you dare think that I have forgotten about you, sir, because I am going to make sure you are my last appointment. Then we will see who is watching who.'

Natalie was trying to find her way out the basement when she heard footsteps coming towards the door. 'Oh heck, just when I'm trying to escape. Now where am I going to hide?' Natalie kept looking around the basement, but only found out how badly she was trapped. 'Damn!' She looked over to were more old, thick blankets lie on the floor. 'Well, I guess I have to hide under here until they leave. Wait a damn minute, Nat, you don't be running from nobody.' She decided to hide behind the basement door. 'Well, whoever comes into that door, I'm going to make sure I get them before they get me.'

Only... no one entered the basement. Natalie put her ear up against the door so she could detect if anyone was trying to come in. No? She eased the basement door open and leaned her head out gently. She looked around didn't see anyone coming... 'OKay, here is my chance to make a run for it.' Trying to so she suddenly encountered one of the bodyguards coming down the hallway. Natalie jumped back and hid again. When she thought they had come a little closer she came from behind the door and started swinging. The bodyguard had stopped in his tracks and reached for Natalie's long black hair. "Oh no you don't, bitch..." but Natalie swung one of her legs underneath the bodyguard's legs, kicking and punching him down to the floor. She and the bodyguard continued to fight. Jessica immediately ran in to see what caused the commotion.

When she saw what the noise was about Jessica couldn't believe this was happening right in front of her. "How the hell did you get out and lose?"

At that sound Natalie stopped and turned around to see her sister Jessica. She charged at her, but one of Jessica's hitmen jumped in front and tried to protect her. Natalie raised her foot and kicked him dead in his groin, yelling, "If I were you, I would get the hell out of my way!" Suddenly one of the bodyguards came from behind and grabbed Natalie by the throat, bringing her down to her knees. Natalie gasped for air and bent down. In that position Natalie reached inside of her shoe and brought out a small silver device. She swung her arm around and stabbed the tiny pocket knife into bodyguard's leg. Natalie grabbed her throat once again, still trying to get some air. She turned around to looked again to notice that there were more of Jessica's hitmen coming now. "Damn, this bitch will not give up will she?" Natalie got herself together to stand to her feet. Stumbling as she tried to get her balance right, 'OKay Nat, get it together girl,' she took a deep in and exhaled a big cool one. She continued to look for her baby sister. Natalie yelled out, "Jess, I know you are around here somewhere! So why don't you just come out and face me or you are too scared of what I might do to you?"

Natalie kept on walking and yelling through the house. She stopped long enough to notice how everything had gotten quiet. She continued to walk at a slow pace, but suddenly turned a corner into Ted Rogers standing right in front of her. "Oh, so, I guess my little, sweet, ass-kisser sister got you to do her dirty work."

Ted replied by laughing, "You really think that Jessica has me on a tight leash?" They walked around one another, staring each other in the eyes, sizing one another up.

Natalie backed up with her fists balled. "Hell yeah I do. You are like her little black poodle. So tell me, Ted, how many bones did she tell you to go and fetch

He was mad over again. "How about I'll just go ahead and kill you right here and now?"

Natalie laughed with a grin on her face, "Don't flatter yourself. Didn't you already try that once today, Mr. Rogers? And somehow you didn't succeed at . Well, how about you go ahead and try your luck this time again? Because, this time, I think it's about to run out."

They both charged at one another. Natalie knew that this time around she was going to kill him. Ted Rogers pulled out his gun and fired at Natalie twice, but missed her by a mere inch. Natalie dropped to the floor and stretched her leg as far as she could. Ted Rogers fell face down, and the gun fell out of his hand. Natalie quickly picked up the gun and pointed it at him.

"I told you, Ted Rogers, if you were to ever cross me, what I was going to do to you!"

Ted looked at Natalie while she was holding his gun. "Look, I know we got off on the wrong foot, but can't we just work things out?"

Natalie turned her head toward the wall and bit down on her lip. She looked down at Ted and smiled. "Now why in the hell would I do that, huh? Please, enlighten me for heaven sake..."

Ted tried to beg and pleaded with Natalie, but all she was worrying about at that moment was her revenge. Natalie, still looking down at him with no remorse in her heart, "This is going to hurt me as much as this is going to hurt you, though I never did like your funky tail no way." She stepped back and pulled the trigger, shooting Ted Rogers in the head.

That done, she could not wait to catch her beloved baby sister. 'This time when we come face to face, Jessica James, I'm going to made sure that I kill you – no hesitation, no remorse.' Natalie was beginning to feel herself as a cold-hearted killer.

Natalie's phone rang. She looked down at it, and she wondered if it was a trap, but she answered it. "Well, well, well – if isn't the call I've been waiting on." She took the phone away from her ear and put it on speaker.

"Well hello, big sister Natalie."

Natalie huffed at the phone, "What the hell do you want, Jess? Mind you, it doesn't matter what you say or do; I'm still going to kill you. So what is it that you want?"

Jessica laughed. "Nat dear, you are so funny when you want to be. You know that?"

"Look, if you're not calling for me to come kill you, which I'm going to do anyway, then I suggest that you go ahead and hang up because I am done talking."

Jessica laughed a little longer, but a lot harder, "OKay, well since you want to know why I am calling you, you must know that I have your older sibling here with me: sweet, loving Dakota James."

Natalie breathed even harder this time. "Jess I'm telling you now, if you hurt one hair on my... other sister's head, I promise you I'm going to kill you girl."

Jessica yelled back through the phone, "Yeah, yeah whatever, Nat. You are not going to do a damn thing! Besides, she is your sister, not mine. Anyway, like I was saying, I need for you to come to 42 Lexington Drive, and don' t try anything sneaky, either, or I'll kill her."

Natalie's lip curled into a sneer. "Wait, did you say Lexington Drive? That is the street I live on, girl. Please tell me you are not in my house, Jessica!" Natalie was still hollering through the phone, but met silence.

Chapter 19

She got into her car and drove down the street. Natalie thought, 'How the hell did she get into my house? ... Or is she even at my house? This better not be one of her scams that she is pulling.' The more Natalie thought about Jessica the angrier she got. Natalie's phone rang again, "Hello who is this?" and once again all she heard was complete silence. She took the phone away from her ear and looked at it and frowned. 'OKay, what the heck was that about?

She pulled up at her condo into her driveway. Natalie got out of her car and peered around. She took a deep breath. 'Now where the hell is she?' Natalie took out her phone and returned the.

"OKay! Jess, where are you? I'm here now, you can let Dakota go."

Jessica just laughed over the phone for a good moment, then replied, "Not until you come inside so we can have a little chit-chat."

Natalie *** away from the phone. "A little chit-chat? Girl, I don't even know where your crazy ass is at. And another thing, how do I know this isn't one of your games you are trying to pull on me again?"

Jessica stepped outside, but on Mr. Lincoln's porch. Natalie spun her head towards Jessica. She was completely shocked by what she was seeing; What the hell is she doing coming out of Mr. Lincoln's house? Jessica strode towards Natalie. "Well, are you going to come inside or what? I don't have all day you know."

Natalie tilted her head and made a huh sound, "You could have fooled me, with all the damn acting you've been doing lately."

Jessica turned her back on Natalie and walked away. Entering Mr. Lincoln's House, Natalie certainly got a weird feeling. Jessica pulled out her own gun and kept it on Natalie, patting her down well.

"Wait, what the hell is this about?" Natalie's face showed her confusion. "You mean to tell me that your lucky charm, green apple self is going to frisk me when your ass could have done that shit outside? OKay, Jessica, what's really going on here?

Jessica smiled, "Well big sis, like I told you before I'm in charge, and I wanted you dead."

Natalie stepped back and just looked at her sister up and down. "Well that's too damn bad because I'm not going anywhere. Look, I didn't come here to be playing around... with or your rent-a-cops over here. So why don't you give me my sister, and we can be on our way out of here?"

Jessica walked a circle around Natalie, while looking her over and smiling. "You really think that I'm going to let the both of you walk out of here alive? Come on Nat, I thought you were smarter than that."

Natalie wished that she had laser eyes so she could kill her sister Jessica right on the spot. "OKay now, Jess, you got me in here so where is Dakota?"

Before Natalie could say anything more Mr. Terry Lincoln entered holding Dakota firmly by the arm. "Let go of me, you dirtbag!" Mr. Lincoln pushed her on the floor at Natalie's feet. She just couldn't believe that her next door neighbor had teamed up with her deceitful sister. Dakota ended up catching her balance right before she hit the floor. Natalie crouched over next to her youngest sister's side to help her up.

"What the hell is wrong with you pushing her like that. I should have known it was something fishy about you."

Just adding to the strangeness of the situation Mr. Lincoln looked at Natalie and smiled and said, "I'm going to need you to shut your mouth before I shut it for you." Then he walked a little closer to Natalie, and grabbed her long black hair.

Natalie snatched her head back as hard as she could. "Don't be putting your nasty-ass hands on me. And besides, unless you are going to get my hair done again, mister, I suggest you don't touch it, bitch."

Mr. Lincoln was about to step towards Natalie again, but his son – Jerry Cole – had stepped into the room.

"That's enough, dad, let her go. Besides, I want to have the pleasure of killing them both."

Natalie turned and looked back over at Mr. Lincoln and then over at Jerry. "Wait a damn minute, you mean to tell me that this asshole is your son... and this nosy box over here is your daddy?!"

Jerry and Mr. Lincoln smiled back at Natalie in answer. "Oh you see, sweetheart, there is more where that came from."

Natalie leaned her head back once again, seemingly exasperated, "What the hell are you talking about, Mr.-I-can-pull-any-woman-I-want?"

Jerry got closer to Natalie and her sister Dakota with a look upon his face as if he didn't have a care in his body. "Well, you see, Ms. James, long before I meet you I came across a young lady that had a beautiful short hair cut–"

Natalie took a deep breath, "Yeah yeah, yada yada... Get on with it. You're making me bored over here."

Jerry stopped with his polite conversation and turned with a light grin. "Well since you put it that way and you don't want to hear my story... I am your brother-in-Law, and I am married to your sister Jessica."

Natalie dropped her jaw and looked at Jerry quizzically. "Say what? You married to who's sister? Wait, come again. Not that crazy bitch in there?!" Natalie pointed her finger towards the living room, "You really had to be desperate to go and mess with that dingbat?"

Jerry just contented himself with smiling. "You know, you are right, I love that dingbat and you should, too."

Dakota snidely laughed at Jerry's comment. "So what are you telling us this for, because my sister told you to tell us, or do you have a mind of your own? It's not like we care anything that you are married to a psychopath..." Dakota kept right on talking about how crazy her sister Jessica was. Jerry's eyes appeared to turn red in anger as if he were the devil himself.

Natalie caught his enraged looks. "I can't give a rat's ass who you are married to, or why. What I do care about," Natalie walked a little closer to where Jerry where standing, "is that you lied to me, and you have held my sister Dakota for ransom. Also what you're not going to do—"

Before Natalie could finish her sentence Jerry cut her off, "Enough, I've just about had enough of you too whining about how evil your sister is. Don't you see how any of this is going to play out if you'd just go ahead and die?" Natalie and Dakota turn and look at one another with their faces looking more confused than ever.

Natalie let out a light laugh as she backed up from Jerry. "Wow, you are crazy. Not only does she have to do crimes and kill people for her, but you have really lost your entire mind for her."

Jerry simply smiled and walked away, stopping in the doorway to say, "You shouldn't have taken the job to become a hitwoman."

Natalie frowned and looked at him, "And what the hell is that supposed to mean?"

By this time Jessica was reentering the room. "Well OKay, my two big sisters, who will I kill first?" Jessica feigned politeness. She then stalked around the both of them very slowly with a light, beautiful smile upon her face. Her eyes squinted studiously, and Dakota rocked side to side. Jessica cut her eyes over at Natalie. "Oh, there is no need to look like this my beloved sisters. Either way, you both are going to die."

Dakota stopped rocking and looked at Jessica. "Girl, you can't even beat a damn fly. The only reason why you got Natalie and me is because we all thought your little red ass was in some type of trouble. You little damn brat!" Dakota reached for Jessica.

"Oh, I really don't think you want to do that, sis." Jessica stepped back and pulled up her gun. "You must think I'm some kinda of fool, don't you Dakota?"

Dakota scowled, "No, what I do think that you are a big *jackass*."

Natalie burst out with a big, loud laugh, "Oh shit, she called you a big *jackass*."

Jessica was still holding the gun pointed at both of them. "Please don't play me with me. You know damn well that I can defeat the both of you too any day."

Natalie slowly started to slide over to her left, getting a little closer to Jessica. "Oh yeah! We just have to see about that, now won't we?"

Jessica and Natalie began to grapple with one another.

Dakota quickly jumped in front of both of them. "OKay, you know what? I've just about had enough of you!" And she came across Jessica's face with her hand.

Jessica stumbled back from the hit as if a bolt of lighting had struck her. "Bitch are you crazy, how dare you hit me in my face?!" Jessica raised the gun and hit Dakota over the head with it, knocking her down onto the floor. Jessica turned around and looked back at Natalie, "OKay bitch, you're next!" but by the time she went to reach for Jessica's face Mr. Lincoln had came back into the front room.

"May I ask what the heck is going on here?"

Jessica kept looking at Natalie, then looked down at Dakota as if she wanted her two sisters dead. Natalie stooped to check that Dakota was alright. She turned and looked back up at Jessica.

"This is not over by a long shot, you damn bitch. You go ahead and laugh if you want to, but I'm telling you, Jess, I am coming back for you."

Jessica regarded Natalie as if she were crazy. "And who said you were even leaving this house, Miss James?"

Natalie, helping her sister Dakota up from off the floor, said back at both Jessica and Mr. Lincoln, "This isn't over by a long shot, and as for you, Mr. Nosy-neighbor, count your fucking days; you are going to be the first one on my hit list."

Jessica turned her head and looked back at Mr. Lincoln with a look as if she was starting to get scared. "What are you doing? You just can't let her walk out of here like that. Are you crazy? What the hell do I pay you for? If you are just going to let her get away–"

Mr. Lincoln turned his head and laughed at Jessica. "Oh, trust me she is not going to get far, all I have to do is just sit back and wait." With a big smile on his face, that said he just knew that he had Natalie in the palms of his hands.

Chapter 20

Natalie left Mr. Lincoln's house still trying to hold Dakota up with one hand and yet hold the gun in the other. Finally it became unbearable and too awkward, "OKay girl, I'm going to need you to hold yourself up." However, Dakota was drifting in and out of consciousness. It seemed the more effort she needed from her sister the less Dakota was able to perform. Natalie shook her sister as hard as she could. "Look dammit, I need you wake up or they're going to kill us both! Do you understand me, Dakota?" Suddenly gunshots were fired seemingly out of nowhere.

Hunkering down behind her car, Natalie mumbled, "What the hell is that?" under her breath. She draped her arm it over Dakota's body, and she scanned around ready to fire back. When she looked, slowly peeking her head around the car to try and see where the shots were coming from, she didn't see anyone.

"OKay, stinking ass, if you want me then I suggest that you come and get me!" Natalie poked her head out again, but this time she managed to catch sight of her old partner, Ryan Jackson. Natalie duck back down. "Damn!" she muttered again, "What the hell is he doing here? Don't tell me he's out to kill me, too."

Natalie thought worriedly to herself even when her old partner hollered out, "Hey Natalie, are you OKay?" So the more he yelled, the less she felt she should say anything. "Come on, Nat! It's me, Ryan, your partner for crying out loud! Girl, if your little ass doesn't say anything, I will kill you."

Natalie yelled back, "How do I know you are not with them, and that this is a setup so you can kill me and my sister Dakota?"

Ryan had to paused for several pulse beats. "Wait! Dakota is with you... I thought you were by yourself." While talking he kept looking around to see from where her voice came. "Wait... look, girl,

I am not going to keep yelling over this damn parking lot. Where the hell are you... so I can help you...?"

Natalie continued yelling across the parking lot. "Yeah, that's the same damn thing my brother Tip said, until he tried to kill me!"

Ryan, looking confused, couldn't believe what had just come out of Natalie's mouth. "Natalie, what the hell are you talking about Girl? I am here to help you, not hurt you. You know me better than that..."

Natalie was still trying to catch sight of him by looking over the car. She could hear his voice, but where... until Ryan came up behind her and grabbed her hand with the gun. "Look, I'm not here to hurt you, Nat." Ryan and Natalie began to wrestle over the gun, him finally succeeding at prying the gun out of Natalie's hand. "Damn, Girl! You really are a strong bitch!" Ryan held his hand out to help Natalie off the ground. "Now are you going to tell me what is really going on here?"

She turned and looked back at her sister Dakota then over at Ryan, "It's Jessica's dusty ass. She wants to kill me, and take over the business that I thought was Ted Rogers'."

Ryan was looking even more confused than he had been at their brief yelled exchanges. "Wait, what are you talking about? Your sister is what again..."

Natalie glared impatiently at him while taking in deep breaths. "Will you keep up with what I'm trying to tell you, damn?"

Ryan had stepped back away from the car while looking at Dakota covered in blood. "What the hell happened to Dakota?"

Natalie shook her head, "You don't listen for shit, do you? I specifically said that my crazy ass sister Jessica is trying to kill me! Do you understand me now Ryan?" Ryan went to open his mouth and say something else, but Natalie cut him off. "And don't ask why either? I've been asking that same damn question all day in my head. I just need to get Dakota to the hospital before she dies – I can't have that on my hands," still between heaving breaths, "but I do know, I'm going to kill my sister Jessica and everything that's behind her."

Ryan's eyes grew huge. "OKay, Nat, you are starting to scare me, and I don't scare that easily."

Natalie batted her eyes as she looked at Ryan and smiled, "Good ... somebody needs to be scared of me. Because if they're not, I'm going to make damn sure that they are."

Ryan leaned his head, with a frown, "Girl, what the hell! You have really has lost your damn mind, Natalie. Look, I don't know what's going on but you need to calm down before you end up killing your own damn self."

Natalie leaned back onto the car and cried. "I just can't believe my own sister wants me dead. The nerve of her, after all I put myself through and she is going to do this crap to me. That little red bitch." Natalie took her hand and swung it at the car's window.

Ryan jumped back, his hands held out to deflect. "Hey! Wait a minute now, I know you are upset, but breaking your car window is not going to solve anything, Natalie. Look, let's go ahead and take your sister to the ER, and then we can try to figure something out. OKay... can you do that for me?" With his hand still outstretched Ryan started inching closer to Natalie. He reached out to give her a big hug. "Girl, your ass is crazy, but in the meantime we need to hurry up and get your sister to the hospital, 'cause she is not looking too good at all."

Natalie stepped back from Ryan and looked down at Dakota. "Oh my God, we have to get a move on!" They both got into the car, but then Michael Fisher seemed to come out of nowhere and fire his gun at them. They both ducked their heads as Natalie put the car into reverse. While she backed the car up from its space Ryan pulled his gun and fired back.

"What the hell is going on Nat, and why are they shooting at us?"

Natalie turned her head as quickly as she could, to look at Ryan as if he had just asked a dumb question. "Really? You're going to ask me why they are shooting at us? Apparently you didn't hear one damn thing I said back there!"

Ryan kept shooting back at Micheal, but took a second to turn and look at Natalie, "No I didn't because it's not making any sense!"

Natalie shook her head and continued driving. She looked up at the rearview mirror, to see if Michael Fisher was still behind them. Then Natalie turned back at Ryan and asked, "Are you going to listen now, or are you just going to pretend that you are listening?" Ryan looked back at Natalie and shrugged, "Well hell, it doesn't look like I have a choice now, do I?"

Natalie looked at him again and laughed, "No you don't, but I will say thank you for helping me and my sister Dakota. I'm going to need you to help take down my other sister. Can you do that for me?"

Ryan turned and looked back at Dakota. "Yeah, I will help you, but on one condition."

Natalie pulled up at the hospital and turned back toward Ryan, not sure about what he was going to ask her. "OKay, what is that you need for me to do?"

Ryan closed his eyes. "Just make sure that whatever goes down tonight, let's make sure we do a hell of a full ride going out."

Natalie turned her head and smiled. "You know I got your back, just as much as you have mine."

When they tried to get Dakota out of the car the young sister spit heavy blood out of her mouth. She turned and looked up at Natalie, "I can't do this, please leave me. I'm going to die anyway."

Natalie and Ryan carried Dakota into the hospital supporting her from under her arms. Natalie yelled out, "I need help, please! Can someone please help my sister, she's coughing up blood!" One of the doctors ran over to help.

"OKay everyone, we got this. I need the both of you to step back so we can do our jobs."

Natalie's first reaction was, "Who the hell do you think you are talking to?"

Ryan pulled Natalie by her arm. "Look, let's not made a scene, let them do their jobs. And besides, we have a bigger problem than this. Your sister Jessica remember."

Natalie turned and looked at Ryan as if he had lost his mind. "Well, I guess you are right," Natalie visibly calmed down, "but I still want to make sure she is going to be OKay."

Ryan turned his head to look back over at Dakota, as they were wheeling her into the back. "I think she is going to be just fine. Besides they have lots of security, and good doctors around this place." Ryan looked back at Natalie as he started to shake. "This place is starting to give me the creeps, I hate hospitals."

As they walked towards the exit Natalie's phone rang. She looked down at it then back over at Ryan.

"Well, isn't it about time you call? So now who else are you going to send to try to kill me? I tell you what: why don't you come and try and kill me, and see how that plays out? Natalie chuckled, but the phone fell silent. "Well, I guess she didn't like that conversation too well. What do you think Ryan: should we go and get that conversation she promised me?"

Ryan just smiled.

Later on that night Ryan and Natalie went back to her condo.

"Well, since we are going to kill my sister, I at least thought we might need to take a bath and change our clothes." Ryan turned and walked a little closer to her.

"Now you're talking my kind of language." Natalie held her hand out as she stopped him in his tracks.

"No Sir, it's not that type of party going on around here, and besides, you're going to take your shower first." Natalie handed

Ryan the washcloth and towel. "Get to it! And don't be in there all day, either. We have some unfinished business, we have to take care of." Natalie then contemplated, 'I wonder why my sister really wants to kill me.'

She walked up stairs to her bedroom and addressed her mirror, 'OKay Nat, now why on earth would this brat little sister of yours want you dead so badly.' Natalie frowned even harder in concentration, but was getting confused, 'This can't be because I know more than her, or is it that I have gained respect and she doesn't like the fact that I have more control than she does?' Natalie stared back from her mirror and smiled. 'OKay well, since we got that out of the way. Let's see how much damage I can do. Just to let her know who she is dealing with.'

Natalie leaned her head towards her bedroom door. "OKay, I know you have to be finished in the bathroom, Ryan." Natalie's calling was met with silence. She called out his name again, Ryan still didn't say a word. Natalie reached for her gun and tiptoed to the bathroom. She pushed the door open only to find Mr. Ryan singing an old Temptations song. "What the hell is wrong with you? I called you several times. Why didn't you answer me dammit? Come on, get out of the damn shower. I need to take my bath." Natalie was headed toward the bathroom door where she stopped and turned around and looked back at Ryan, "You damn Luther Vandross wannabe ass."

Ryan looked at Natalie as if she had lost her mind.

Chapter 21

Later that night Natalie packed an overnight bag, however, this wasn't an away bag. When she arrived down stairs Natalie tossed the bag at Ryan's feet noisily.

"What the hell do you have in here, guns?"

Natalie slightly turned her head and smiled. "What? I know you didn't think that I was going to go empty handed…" Natalie was still smiling at Ryan as if she didn't have a care in the world. "Now, how about we go and have some fun with that little brat sister of mine? Oh, and don't forget to call the hospital; I need to know how my sister Dakota is doing."

Ryan nodded at Natalie. "OKay, what is your plan on taking down your sister and the crew that she has working for her?"

The more Natalie thought about how to take down her sister the more she got upset. She paced back and forth around in her front room. 'Damn, why does this have to be this way? I mean – if only she would have come to me and let me know she had a problem with me.' Natalie felt as if her sister had declared war on her. Even though Natalie felt that this was her baby sister, and she knew that she could take her on at any time, this was not be the fight that Natalie really wanted to give up. 'Well let's see if anyone is coming out of Mr. Nosy-ass-neighbor's house.' Natalie went to her patio window and looked out. Ryan frowned at her nervousness and shook his head as if he was sure of who the nosy neighbor really was.

"OKay, so how long do we have to be all 'I-Spy' or, shall I say, playing detective?"

Natalie looked back over at him as if she wanted to punch his lights out. "Why don't you just shut the hell up and focus on who is trying to come out of that house?"

Natalie and Ryan continued to window-sit for movement at Mr. Lincoln's house. Ryan eventually got frustrated. "Look, why are we still just sitting here? I mean – why don't we just go and kick his damn door in, and take back what's yours?"

Natalie whipped her head around and looked at him in a strange way. "Um, because It's not that simple: She has multiple bodyguards over that place, and besides I know just how I want to do it."

Ryan continued to look at her as if she really has gone crazy. "OKay well, I am not just going to sit here all damn night and not do something. I mean, for crying out loud: they almost killed your younger sister.

Natalie jumped to her feet, and confronted Ryan as if she was about to turn her into a mad woman. "And what the hell does that suppose to mean?! Are you suggesting that I'm not going to get my revenge on them?! Is that what you are saying?! Don't forget that bitch shot at me and even had my brother lie to me! Now I've had to kill his ass too!" Natalie still regarded Ryan with eyebrows raised.

Ryan stepped a little back from Natalie. "Wait! You did what? You killed your brother because he lied to you?! Girl, do you have a damn soul in your body? I mean, you're telling me that you just killed your brother, and you don't mind killing again," Ryan looked as confused as ever, "So, if I even thought of crossing you one time... you would probably kill me next, right?

Natalie smiled at Ryan to begin her answer, "I wouldn't even give you the satisfaction to even try to cross me, and if you got that in your mind now, don't! I'll promise you what I might do if you did. They might not even recognize who you are." Natalie walked a little closer to Ryan, leaned over and gave him a kiss on the jaw. "Now can we get back to watching my neighbor's house?" Ryan stared agape at Natalie.

"No, we can't just keep watching your damn neighbor's house, and another thing; What are you so damn mean for, Natalie?"

She twisted her lips one side to the other in thought. "You right, Ryan, I am mean as fuck, but that doesn't stop me from protecting what's mine, does it?"

Ryan's phone rang.

He looked down at it, then back up at Natalie. "I don't recognize the number." He handed his phone over to Natalie.

Suddenly three gunshots crashed though her patio window. Ryan grabbed Natalie and threw her on the floor. Natalie reached for her gun and tried to fire back. "Now you see why I have a damn badass attitude; People are really trying to kill me! You think I'm going to let that happen?" Natalie stood up, to empty her gun clip of shells. She turned and looked down Ryan, but before she could ask he had jumped up empty his ration of shells out also. Be sure you do less talking and more shooting, please?"

"I promise, I will hear your family story another time, but right now we have bodies we have to take down!"

Natalie nodded her head. Suddenly, however, the guns sounds completely stopped. They both peeked their heads out to see if anyone was going to fire back. "OKay, I guess the coast is clear." Ryan and Natalie slowly came from behind the sofa.

They looked around the condo, and Natalie's face twisted up as she started to look at what had happened to her home.

"Will you just look at this mess they made? Oh, I'm definitely going to kill her little red ass now." The more Natalie looked at her house's damage, the madder she got. "Will you just look at my $25,000 home; what the hell was she thinking?!"

Ryan had to step back and began to put up one finger. "Uh... well, technically, Natalie see, she was trying to kill you, but she didn't. So now is your chance to go and kill her. So how about it?" Ryan turned and looked back over at Natalie and smiled.

Natalie's face still showed only rage. "Oh you bet your ass I'm going to make sure I'm going to kill her, and anything that's following down behind her!" Natalie reloaded her gun. She turned back to Ryan with that unpleasant look upon her face, "So are you coming, or are you going to sit this one out?"

Ryan gave Natalie a crazy look. "Sit this one out?! Girl, you got to be out of your head. I told you that I got your back no matter what and, plus, I owe her ass for shooting at me, too." Abruptly he walked out the door, but stopped long enough to look back at Natalie and ask, "Well! Are you coming or not? We have some unfinished business with Miss Jessica James."

They both eased their way over to Mr. Lincoln's condo. Natalie noticed how the front door cracked open a little. She turned around and squinched her eyes tightly at Ryan. She knew something was not right. Natalie pointed her finger at the front door and delicately pushed it open. Natalie and Ryan walked in, but only to find Micheal Fisher standing there waiting with a gun.

"I told you it smell kinda of fishy in here."

Micheal Fisher looked over at Natalie then back over at Ryan. He laughed at the both of them with his gun still trained at them, "Well if you smell something fishy then why did you enter, Miss James?"

Natalie didn't feel as if he was even a target. She knew it would be over for Mr. Fisher with one shot. "Do you really think that I am supposed to be threatened by you and your toy gun? Think again, sir."

Micheal just kept smiling. "You, on the other hand, are not a threat either, Miss James. Besides who are you to say I won't kill you first?"

Natalie leered at Micheal, "Because you already know what type of woman I am, so don't even try and play with me, Mr. Fisher." Natalie pointed her gun at him. "I'm going to only ask you this one time, and one time only; Where is the hell my sister Jessica. I promise you this, if you so much as lie to me, about her whereabouts, oh trust me, I'm going to kill you right here and now."

Micheal coldly looked back at Natalie, than at Ryan. "OKay, and what If I don't tell you where she is?"

Natalie stepped a little further toward him, still pointing the gun at his chest. "Wrong answer, sir!" Natalie pulled the gun trigger and fired her gun point blank at Micheal Fisher's head. "I told you I'm not the one to be playing with."

Natalie and Ryan began look around for Jessica's hiding place, but ran into more of Jessica's bodyguards.

Ryan smiled over at Natalie. "Well, I guess they want a piece of the action, too, huh? So why don't we just go ahead and give them what they came for?"

After they fought Jessica's bodyguards off, Natalie still had to wonder where she could be hiding. She directed, "I'm going to check upstairs, you check the kitchen, and don't forget to look into the closets." Even after a thorough search there was no Jessica to be found.

Natalie strode back down the stairs slowly wondering again how the hell her sister got away so quickly. Natalie walked towards the living room where she could see Ryan standing, but as she entered the room Ryan had this look upon his face as if he knew this was going to be a setup for Natalie. Ryan handed over a piece of paper with Natalie's name on it.

"What the hell is this, and where did you get it from?"

Ryan simply pointed to the coffee table.

"Why would they leave a note with my name on it, but with no address or telephone number?" The confusion crossed her face. "Look, did anyone come in or out of that front door that you know of?"

Ryan shook his head, "No, I haven't seen or heard from anyone. I tell you, Natalie, something is very fishy, and it's not adding up to why your sister wants you dead."

Natalie's phone started to ring. "Oh my God! It's my mom. Why would she be calling me around this time of night?" She answered the phone, "Hello! Mom, how are you? Are you OKay? You don't need anything do you?" Natalie looked more confused than ever at her mother Jackie James screaming through the phone. Natalie had to hold the phone away from ear. Then she tried to get a word in, but her mother kept right on yelling through the phone. "Mom... mom... OKay mom, please... Can I please get a word out so I can tell you what really happened?" However, Natalie's mother was really not trying to hear a thing she had to say. Natalie decided she had to hang up on her mother while she was still talking.

Ryan coked his head and looked at Natalie in a weird way. "Uh, please tell me that you just didn't hing upon your mother..."

Natalie threw back her not giving two rats' asses expression. "Yes, I did hang up on my mother. She wouldn't let me get a word in edgewise, so I hung on her, Ryan"

He smiled, "You know you are going to hell for that, right?"

Natalie looked at Ryan and started to laugh. "Boy, my black ass is already in hell. Now let's go and find that sister of mine me so she can be in hell right along with me."

Ryan shook his head.

Chapter 22

"Well! I would like to know where the hell has she gotten to!" With her next harsh breath she added, "I hate not knowing, but when I get my damn hands on her I'm going to kill her," she looked skyward, "Lord, I just want to know one thing; If I kill her right now please don't hold me accountable for those actions, because this little heifer has done way more than I have!"

Ryan studied Natalie as if she was telling a lie, then realized he knew better. Suddenly Natalie's phone rang yet again.

"Oh my God, What is it now, mom?" She uttered before picking up and then, when she actually answered her phone, "Hello, Mom, what can I do for you?" Natalie raised her hand and formed a gabbing puppet to demonstrate that her mother was getting on her nerves. Natalie switched her mother onto speaker phone. It seemed all there was to hear was a continuous loud stream of tones shouting out, and now she was getting on Ryan's last nerves, too. Now, with new understanding, he shook his head and walked away. Natalie hang up the phone again. She looked back over at Ryan in a pitiful way. "Why does she always want to fuss at me? Why don't you just put me out of my misery?"

Ryan laughed, "What the hell was she screaming about this time, and why?"

Natalie was still looking at him as if she wanted to cry out for help. "I don't fucking know, but I do know if she calls my phone one more damn time I am going to hand the bitch over to you."

Ryan stepped back. "No the hell you won't. I done heard the way that lady talks. She does not let you get one single word in, Jack. So, no, I'm good. Thank you for the invite."

Natalie turned and looked over at Ryan squinching her eyes as if she wanted to hit him next. "OKay well, we are going back to Ted Rogers house. I know for sure Miss Thing is over there waiting."

They got back into the car. Natalie had noticed that the hospital hadn't called her.

Ryan glanced over at Natalie, "What's wrong? Why are you looking like that? Did you forget to say something to your mother?"

"No, I didn't," Natalie glanced back over with a look in her eyes. She knew that Jessica was going after their older sister Dakota next, "Come on we have to get to the hospital before Jessica and her wanna-be bodyguards do." Natalie dialed her mother's number back, but all it did was ring. She took the phone away from her ear and looked back down at it. "OKay, this is not like my mom, she normally answers her phone."

Ryan looked back at Natalie. "OKay, I'm quite sure that your mother is alright, and I'm going to need you to slow the hell down before we get into a damn accident." Natalie kept on driving as if she were manic. Ryan continued to hold on to the car dashboard as if holding on for dear life. "If you don't mind, can you please tell me where the hell are we going before I get car sick."

She continued driving faster than his tastes. "You will see when we get there. As a matter of fact, we are going to my mother's house." Natalie looked at him once again and grinned. "Have you ever been to Suffolk, Virginia?"

Ryan's eyes got big, as if they were brightly colored candies. "What the hell do you mean – are we going to Suffolk? Girl, what the hell is wrong with you? You can't just be springing things on me like that!"

"Boy, you are going to learn today, and besides, you're going to love it there."

They arrived at Natalie's mother's house. Ryan glanced over at Natalie with, "Now what?"

She leaned her head back and looked at him with a frown. "What the hell do you mean 'now what?' We are going into my mother's, that's what." Natalie got out of the car. She noticed that both Jessica's and Mr. Lincoln's cars were sitting out front. "Well I'll be damned! What the hell are they doing over here?"

Natalie and Ryan entered the house. Natalie's mother was sitting at the dining room table.

"Well! Come in my dear, have a set, take a load off."

Natalie looked suspiciously around the room for Jessica, but there was no sign of her anywhere. Jackie looked over at Natalie then glanced over at Ryan.

"OKay, can you tell me why are you two here – and what is it that you could possibly want?" Everyone in Suffolk Va. who knew Jackie James called her Lady James, and they also knew that when it came to dealing with her you've got hell on your hands.

Natalie walked a little closer to her Mother. "OKay, mom, why the hell is Mr. Lincoln and the rest of his crew parked outside of your house?

Jackie smiled at Natalie with an unnerving and not-so-innocent look. "Are you questioning me about who is in my house?" Natalie stepped back from her mother, as Jackie started to stand up. "How the hell are you going to come into my house and ask a question as if your black ass stays here?"

Natalie looked at Ryan then back at her mother. "Yes, I am questioning you on it because your other daughter and her gang are trying to kill me."

Jackie walked away from Natalie, then she turned back around and leveled a stare at her. "Little Girl! First of, I don't think your sister is trying to kill you. And another thing, what the hell is wrong with you with thinking someone is out to get your ass? You need to stop being so damn paranoid."

Natalie furrowed her brow. "What the hell? I can't believe that you think that I'm lying to you. My God! She really has you wrapped around her little finger. Mom, Mr. Lincoln is helping her."

Jackie walked over to where she was standing and came across Natalie's face with her right hand. "You will not talk about your sister or the man of my life in any kinda of way!"

Natalie looked back at Ryan and then her mother. "You crazy bitch, I can't believe you just hit me!"

"Yes I did, and I will do it again!"

Natalie was still in shock that her mother didn't even believe her about her sister Jessica, and compounded by the fact that she had hit her and all Natalie could think to do was laugh at her mother, "You know what, Jackie James, if you ever hit me like that again I will kill you myself; And that's not a threat, that is a promise." Natalie went to walk out of the dining room. When she stopped to think to herself, 'I can't believe that she thinks I am lying to her. And how the hell did she hook up with Mr-two-timing Lincoln. That's OKay, she'd better be lucky her ass is my mother or her ass would be lying right next to her damn son, Tip. OKay Nat, calm down and get yourself together and find that no-good-ass sister of yours, and prove to your mother that you were right all along.'

Ryan stepped in front of Natalie. "Uh, Nat, are you OKay? I mean, I can take you to the hospital and they can treat you for mental health issues... You do know that right?" Natalie turned her head very slowly and looked at Ryan as if he was the one with the mental issues.

"Boy, I'm fine. I just need to try and convince my mother that my baby sister is trying to kill me. Hey, and another thing, why the hell didn't you say anything? Your ass was right there. When she was trying to kill me, you ass bucket."

Ryan was still looking at Natalie as if she had really lost it. "Me? What do you mean me? And yes, I was there but I done already told you that I am not going to say anything to your crazy momma."

Natalie rolled her eyes. "You make me sick, you know that?"

Ryan smiled at her, "Yeah, but in a good way."

"Will you come on and let's go? I have to see how can I get Mr. Lincoln out of my mother's house so I can kill him."

Ryan simply replied, "Yep! You're crazy."

Natalie rolled her eyes again while smacking her lips. "Boy! Will you shut up and help me think of a plan so I can get his ass out of here?" However Natalie's upset just deepened the more she thought on it. "Damn! There has got to be away," then suddenly Natalie got the idea, "What if I go after his son Jerry Cole? That just might get him to come out." Natalie continued to smile when she looked over at Ryan. "Well, I think I just might have a plan."

Ryan frowned. "What are you talking about Natalie?"

She looked at him with one eyebrow up and a light grin on her face. Natalie just knew it, that her plan might help her get revenge on her sister. "Well, come on so we can go and check on my sister Dakota. I want to make sure that she is doing OKay."

Ryan was still looking as confused as ever. "Yeah, but you didn't tell me what is your plan? Just how are you going to get your revenge on your sister if you don't tell me what's going on?"

"I will tell you what's going on later, but right now we have to see how my Dakota is doing." She and Ryan arrived at the hospital, where Natalie walked up toward a nurse's station. "Hello, I'm here to see Dakota James. Can you please tell me what room she is in?" The nurse turned around and looked at Natalie as if she stank.

"Well damn, lady, can you please give me my sister's room number before I flip the cowboy shit out on you?" Natalie banged on the counter with her balled up her hands.

Ryan jumped in front of Natalie pulling her by the arm over to the other side of the room as he started to whisper, "Look! If you want to see your sister then I suggest you put a sock into that attitude you got." Natalie snatched her arm away.

In her soft angry voice and her lips folded in, Natalie growled, "I'll tell you one thing, mister, if she doesn't tell me where the hell my sister is... hell is going to break loose up in here," Natalie walked away, she looked back at Ryan, "and keep your damn hands off of me." They walked over to the nurse station for a second time. Natalie took in a deep breath, "Well, I'm sorry about early. Could you please tell me what room my sister is in?"

The nurse still looked at Natalie as if she was never going to give her any information. She simply turned her back and walked away. Natalie stared at Ryan with eyes as big as fifty cent pieces.

"That bitch! OKay you want to keep playing with me," Natalie jumped across the nurse's station counter grabbing for the nurse, "bitch, you're going to tell me where my sister is!"

Before Ryan could reach his hand out to stop Natalie she had already grabbed the nurse by the hair. "Will you let this woman go?! Girl, let her go!" they both fell on the floor. Natalie got up and tried to charge at the nurse again with Ryan still holding on to her

Natalie began kicking and screaming, "I want to see my sister now! Take your damn hands off of me!" Ryan tried to look up, while he pinned Natalie down to the Floor.

He yelled out, "Natalie stop! For crying out loud you're making a big scene. And, plus, the police are on their way over here."

They both got up off the floor as the off-duty police officer walked over towards them. Natalie and Ryan kept looking down to pretend that they were looking for something on the floor. "Well, honey, I don't see your contacts anywhere. Are you sure you were wearing them?"

Natalie played along with Ryan's lead, "Yes, dear, I could have sworn I put them into my eyes this morning." The police officer got closer to them and asked if they were OKay, "Ma'am, sir are you two alright?"

Ryan looked at Natalie then back at the officer, "Yessir, we are OKay. Just trying to see if my honeybear over here is OKay."

Natalie's eyes began to open up big as if she wanted to shoot him, however his ruse did convince the police officer to leave. Still Natalie turned around and reared up at Ryan. "If you ever call me your honeybear again I promise you my sister won't be the only one worried about me killing them – you'll be next, Ryan!"

He gulped a hard swallow down his throat.

Chapter 23

They eased their way to the back of the hospital. Natalie and Ryan began to find themselves in the computer room. "I'm going to check and see if I can pull up any files on her," Natalie nodded to Ryan, "I'm going to need you to be my look out, and make sure nobody's coming." She looked up Dakota's files and found something very disturbing. "Oh my God," with tears in her eyes, Natalie looked up at Ryan shaking her head; she couldn't believe what she had just read, "No, this can't be true, not my sister. How am I supposed to function without her?"

Ryan looked pleadingly over at Natalie, confused. "What? What is it? What did you see?"

Natalie burst into actual tears, and Ryan moved over to comfort Natalie for support. Natalie fell to her knees. "Why did this have to happen to my sister?" Ryan held Natalie even tighter as she continued to cry.

"Look, I need you to get yourself together. We still have to find out why your other sister Jessica is trying to kill you, Natalie."

She wiped at her face. "Yes, you are right, but I just, –" but before she could even finish her sentence Ryan cut her off. "Look, like I said, you have to focus on one thing at a time. Besides, don't forget that Jerry Cole is married to your sister Jessica. Come on, let's get out of here – we don't want to get caught by the police."

As they as they exited the hospital Natalie turned to Ryan, "We're gonna have to stop at my mother's house for a huge visit with Mrs. Jackie James; One she will never forget."

Ryan looked back over at Natalie with a frown – he knew something was about to go down. When they arrived at Natalie's mother's house, she looked around the front yard. Mr. Lincoln and Jerry's cars weren't absent. So where had the two little-dick bastards gone? Natalie was still sitting in the car as she wondered what would happen next.

Ryan, looking out of the car window, asked, "OKay Nat, What is your next move? I can't help you, if you don't tell me what is really going to happen."

Natalie looked over at Ryan. "My mother, Jackie James, who is better known as Lady James; She deals in shipments, with drugs and jewelry. Have you ever heard of a gang called the 103 Gang?"

Ryan leaned his head over a little further towards the window, then he looked at Natalie as if he had seen a ghost. "Wait, what? You're telling me that your mother is the head leader of the 103 Gang?"

Natalie giggled as she glanced over at him. "Yes, that is exactly what I am trying to say. So, are you going to help me take down my beautiful, intelligent mother?"

Ryan looked as confused as ever. "Yea, on one condition: you have to make sure she never knows where I live."

Natalie laughed, "Yeah, you have my word." Natalie caught a look out of her side view mirror. She could see Mr. Lincoln and Jerry Cole getting out of a car fussing at one another. Natalie nudged Ryan in his side and pointed.

Ryan raised his head. "Oh, so father and son are at each other's throats," Ryan just had to laugh, "I wonder what that is all about?"

Natalie huffed, "I don't know, and I don't care. All I know is that I want my revenge. I couldn't care if they killed each other."

Mr. Lincoln and Jerry walked into the house. Mr Lincoln had yelled out Jackie's name, "Hey Girl, where the hell are you?" However he didn't seem to be getting an answer until Jackie walked out of the kitchen.

"Why in the hell are you calling my damn name like you have lost your mind?!" she walked over to where Lincoln was standing, "I don't know what or who the hell you think you are, but you call my name like that again, and I will kill right where you are standing!"

Lincoln looked at Jerry, then back at Jackie. He burst out laughing. "Well, I wanted to know if you've seen that daughter Natalie today..."

Jackie frowned as she turned to look over at Lincoln for the second time, "Yes, early on. Why? ...And why are you asking about my daughter?" Jackie kept right on looking at him as if she was getting suspicious of him.

"Huh, nothing I just was asking that's all. So are you going to round up all of your gang members? So we can finish up on what we started."

Jackie's suspicious look deepened. " We? What do you mean 'we'? You mean *me* – so I can finish up on what *I* have started..." Jackie ** pointed her finger at Mr. Lincoln. "Don't you dare come into my damn house and try to run shit. You got that?"
Lincoln rolled his eyes. "Yeah, I got it." He turned back to Jerry. "Come on before I end up smacking a bitch in here."

Jackie's brow creased even more. "I know you are not even talking 'bout me. You really must want to die tonight. If you even put your nasty ass hands on me you will be drawing back a nub. Now, Try me Mr. Terry Lincoln."

Terry and Jerry began to leave the house. Natalie looked at the both of them sideways as they get back into their cars. 'You will not get away from what you have done. She drove to follow them back to Mr. Lincoln's house. Natalie looked at Ryan out of the corner of her eyes. "OKay, here is my chance to get my revenge on both of their black asses." Natalie and Ryan began to ease their way into Mr. Lincoln's house, when suddenly Natalie phone's rang. "Dammit!" she responded in her lowest aggressive hiss. "Now who in the hell would call me when I am about to get my kill on?"

Ryan turned Natalie with a frown. "Why on earth would that even come out of your mouth?"

She glared back at him, then smiled. "Hello, who is this?"

Natalie put the cell phone on speaker in time for the voice on the other end, which sounded familiar, "Hello, Nat – are you there? This is Charlette Diamond, Dakota's daughter."

Natalie looked down at her phone and then looked back at Ryan. "You who, again? My sister Dakota doesn't have any children, and besides, if she did, she would have let me, of all people, know. So if you, little girl, are trying to pull a prank on someone: guess again – nice try."

Charlette yelled through the phone, "Wait! My mother said you hate to be called Nattie Pooh or bunny."

Natalie stared at the phone. The more Charlette continued to say the more Natalie was convinced she was Dakota's daughter. "OKay look, I am in the middle of something right now. If you don't mind, can I call you back? ... Or vise versa, which everyone you feel like doing..."

Charlette answered Natalie back, "Of course I would be glad to call you back." Natalie and Charlotte hung up the call.

She looked back over at Ryan. "OKay, now, where was I?" Natalie began to ease her way over toward Mr. Lincoln's house, but Ryan grabbed Natalie by her arm.

"Wait! I think you should wait until they at least come back out. Then we can just fire at them from here."

Natalie turned and just stared at Ryan. In her low voice she whispered, "Are you crazy? What the hell is wrong with you? Why the hell should I wait? Wait for what – for hell to freeze over? Boy, you'd better come on here and help me kill these people, with your non-shooting, scared ass."

Ryan went to open his mouth to say something, but nothing came out of it. Natalie ran toward the house again, but Ryan grabbed her by the arm a second time. Natalie looked back down at her arm then frowned.

"Boy, what the hell is wrong with you? If you don't let me go so I can go in here and do what I have to do..." Natalie snatched her arm away.

Ryan, looking around, noticed that Natalie's mother Jackie was walking up toward the house. "Is this really what you want to do?" He grabbed Natalie again by the arm and pointed toward the house.

Natalie looked up and saw her mother. "What the hell is she doing here?" Not only did she see her mother, but she also saw her father. Natalie's eyes had gotten wide. "Oh hell naw! I know damn well he is not working with her crazy corrupted ass..." She drew a deep breath, then looked back at Ryan. "Now what am I supposed to do? My father is in that house – I can't just go into there and start firing my gun..."

Ryan looked back at Natalie with a look as if he felt her pain. "Your mother is in there, too, what about her, Natalie?"

She turned slowly to look at Ryan as if he was crazy. "Damn her! That's how I'm in the predicament that I'm in now. Oh, she really has to go now!"

Ryan shook his head – he knew Natalie was not playing about killing her mother.

Chapter 24

Even before Natalie could walk in and kill her mother her phone chimed in again. She picked it up, "Hello didn't I tell you that I was busy."

"I know, that's why I am over here now." Natalie turn around to see Charlette stepping into view.

"How the hell did you know where to find me?"

Charlette burst out laughing, "Auntie, it's called a GPS tracking; maybe you should give it a try."

Natalie cocked her head to look at Charlette as if she was crazy. "Look, little girl, I don't know why you are here, but you need to leave right now."

Charlette smiled at Natalie. "You know exactly why I am here, Aunt Nat. I want in on the 103 gang proposition. It is a family business, right? And I am family."

Charlette continued to walk a closer to Natalie. When she did stop, Charlette leaned her body to one hip, continuing to smile.

Natalie walked around Charlette, "Look, I don't know where you are getting your information from, missy, but like I said-"

Before Natalie could even finish her sentence, Charlette cut her off, "It's Miss James, and like I said before I want in, or I'll just walk up to that front door," as she pointed at Mr. Lincoln's house, "so what's It's going to be Auntie Nattie?"

Natalie's eyes narrowed tightly to glare at Charlette Diamond. "I'd prefer you not to call me that, you little ungrateful bitch. Until I really find out if you are my sister's daughter or not I would like for you to call me Miss Natalie."

Charlette looked Natalie up and down with one eyebrow up. "OKay, we will just see about that auntie." Charlette walked up towards the house.

Natalie reached back at Ryan. "This bitch is just as crazy as I am."

The three all walked up towards Mr. Lincoln's house. Charlette turned the knob and walked in. "Hey, is anyone here?" Ryan and Natalie looked at one another and then pulled out their guns.

"You're right Natalie, she's just as crazy as your ass is."

Natalie glared at Ryan as if she really wanted to show him who was crazy. Jackie walked into view across the dining room.

"Yes! Can I help you?" When Jackie got a little closer she noticed that Natalie was standing there. "Oh lord, Nat, what have you done now?"

Natalie looked at her mother with one eyebrow up. "Excuse me, I haven't done a damn thing, yet. Don't you mean to greet your granddaughter over here?" Jackie regarded Natalie as if she had no idea what she was talking about. "Yeah mom! She's supposed to be your granddaughter... but I know that's a lie because Dakota doesn't have any kids."

Before Jackie could say anything Natalie's father, Jonathan Smith, walked into the room saying, "Charlette Diamonds James."

"What the hell? You know her?" Natalie walked around Charlotte to face him, "Wait one damn minute; You mean to tell me that Dakota has a daughter, and no one has told me about it." Everyone looked at one another knowingly. Jonathan walked a little closer to Natalie, but she backed up. "Hell, naw! You have no right to hold any kinda information like this away from me. And another thing..." as she backed over towards her mother Jackie and giggled, "You need to tell your boyfriend and his son that I am coming for them," Abruptly Natalie walked away, "and after I'm done with them I will be back for your ass next."

Jackie's eyebrow went up, "Girl don't you even try that bullshit with me. You forgot, I'm the one who taught you how to fight and hold a damn gun. So if you want a piece of me, Miss Natalie James, my door is always open.

Natalie looked at Jackie and walked away.

Jonathan looked over at Jackie. "Are you going to let her talk to you like that?"

Jackie leaned her head askew once again and looked at her ex-husband. "Like I said, Jon, she knew who to play cards with and who not to play cards with, and apparently she doesn't want to play any cards with me." Jonathan had to wonder if his daughter was actually bluffing or is she was dead serious about killing her own mother.

Charlette Diamond walked over towards her grandparents with questions about joining the family business. "Look, I know y'all don't know me that well, for me to be asking you this..."

Jonathan and Jackie looked at one another and smiled. "What is it baby? Tell us what's on your mind."

Charlette took a deep breath. "Well, I want to be into the family business. My mother told me about what was going on, and I think it's time for me to step in for my mother, ... and you did try to kill her."

Jonathan turned on Jackie with a confused look upon his face. "Wait one damn minute," now looking like he could pull her head off of her body, "I know damn well you didn't come for my baby girl... or any of my children." Jonathan walked closer to Jackie to loom with threat. "Bitch, if I even thought that you were trying to hurt my children I would put your ass in a pin box. Jackie, don't think I am scared of you because I am not." He got closer into Jackie's face. "I'm telling you now: if any of my babies get hurt because of your careless ass I'm going to kill you, woman," he pointed his finger into Jackie's face, "and that's not a threat, it's a promise, bitch." Jonathan stalked away. He stopped and turned next to his granddaughter. "Well, Charlette Diamond, if you want to know about the family business, I will be happy to teach you."

Charlotte smiled.

As Natalie and Ryan left from Mr. Lincoln's house Jerry walked from around the side of the building. "What the hell are you doing coming out of my father's house, bitch?"

Natalie smiled, but continued to walk off of the porch looking Jerry dead in the eyes. "Well, well! You are the person I have been waiting on," Natalie hurried out her gun, and leveled it at Jerry, "so I suggest that you go ahead and say goodbye to your daddy, because I am about to kill you right here and now!"

Natalie and Jerry shot at one another.

Jonathan looked up at Charlette then back at Jackie, "Did y'all hear-"

Suddenly the gun shots got louder and louder. Jackie ran into the bedroom to reach for her gun. She came back to the dining room and pointed at Jonathan. "I think I need to tell you something about our daughter Natalie."

Jonathan looked at Jackie with a frown, "Well, Lady James, whatever you got to tell me – gone to have to wait."

Jackie, trying to tell him what happened that morning, kept right on calling out Jonathan's name.

Finally Jonthan halted his momentum and yelled out, "What the hell do you want, Jackie?!"

Jackie looked at him with tears in her eyes. "That's our daughter out there firing those guns."

Jonathan stepped back and look at Jackie as if she had lost her mind. "And again I am asking you, what the hell are you talking about, Jackie?!"

She proceeded to tell Jonathan what was going on.

Jonathan ran out the front door. With his gun he fired into the air three times.

Natalie and Jerry suddenly stopped firing their guns, to turn around and look at Jonathan, who commanded, "If I were you, I would go ahead and put down your gun before there would be some misunderstanding!"

Jerry, still holding onto the gun, "What?! Do you think I am crazy?! I'm not going to put down my gun."

Jonathan and Jerry remained in a standoff until Mr. Lincoln came running out of the house.

Natalie gestured at Ryan then over to her father, Jonathan. "OKay, Jerry, why don't you go ahead and tell my daddy exactly why you're pointing that gun at his daughter?"

Jerry started to laugh. "What the hell are you talking about, girl? You were trying to kill me," Jerry looked over and saw Mr. Lincoln, his own father, standing there and hollered out, "Tell them, dad, what they are trying to do to us..."

Mr. Lincoln looked back over at Jerry. "Please son, put the gun down." Mr. Lincoln pleaded with Jerry, but Jerry didn't want to listen.

"Naw! Like I said earlier," as he pointed his gun back at Natalie, "I am going to kill your little black ass." Jerry pulled the trigger to fire at Natalie, but only missed her by an inch. Natalie re-aimed her gun and fired back, striking Jerry Cole dead in the head.

Mr. Lincoln yelled out, "No! Not my son! You bitch, do you know what you have just done?"

Natalie looked over at Mr. Lincoln. "Yes I know exactly what I have done. Now you can go inside, and tell your girlfriend that I will be back for her as well." Mr. Terry Lincoln wept and knelt to hold his son. He looked up at Natalie with tears rolling down his face. "I'm going to made sure you pay for what you did. Do you hear me Natalie James? I'm going to made you pay."

She turned around and looked back at Mr. Lincoln. "Like I said: I will be back for you and your mistress."

Jonathan turned around and looked back at Jackie and asked, "Jackie, what the hell are they talking about? Mistress? Are you sleeping with Terry, because if you are I might as well go ahead and kill you myself?

Jackie turned her head to look after Natalie's departing figure and rolled her eyes. "What the hell are you talking about Jon? I am not sleeping with no one, and as far as your daughter went... Like I said before, if she wants to play cards with me she knows exactly where to find me."

Jon looked back over at Mr. Lincoln and then at Jackie. "So help me, if I find out that you have been sleeping together," with a murderous look on his face, "I will kill you both. Mark my words." Jackie and Mr. Lincoln stared at one another as if they hoped that that truth would never come out.

Chapter 25

Jackie turned around and ran behind her husband. "Jonathan, look you have to believe me! I would never betray you in any kind of way," but the look on Jackie's face said otherwise.

Jonathan took in a deep breath and exhaled a hot one out. "Yeah, right! What do you take me for, Jackie? A damn fool, I don't believe a damn word that comes out of your mouth." Suddenly Jonathan's phone lit up with a call. He looked down at it, then back up at Jackie puzzled. "Why is the Lake County hospital calling me?"

He answered, "Hello?" momentarily Jonathan's mouth dropped if he was in a state of shock. He hung up the phone. Tears rolled down his face.

Jackie approached looking at him. "OKay well, what did they want with you, and why are you crying, Jonathan. Please tell me what's going on."

Jonathan looked up at Jackie. "Our little girl Dakota is in the hospital with leukemia. Oh my God! What are we going to do?"

Unexpectedly Jackie smiled. "Good for her, that's one less daughter I have to worry about." Jackie nodded at Jonathan and walked away.

"What the hell you mean, 'Good for her'? That's our daughter here you're talking about!"

Jackie turned around and looked at Jonathan as if she couldn't give two rats' asses. "What the hell are *you* talking about, 'Our daughter'? She is not my daughter, she is yours. I only have one child: Jessica. All I care about is my daughter, Jess. Now if something were to happen to her – Then I would be devastated and heartbroken. Until then, Please do not tell me any little thing about your ratchet-ass children." Jonathan looked after Jackie as she turned and walked away.

Jonathan was still leering at Jackie, "You damn bitch..." Suddenly Jonathan lurched forward and wrapped his hands around Jackie's neck. "I told you the next time you disrespect me or any of my children I was going to kill your ass!"

Jackie struggled get Jonathan's hands from around her neck. She soon felt her breath leaving her body. Things got knocked over in the struggle, but Jonathan was determined that he was going to kill his ex-wife. She looked up to see the bedroom lamp setting on the nightstand. Desperately she reached for it; Jackie took the lamp and struck Jonathan over the head with it. Quickly she crawled her way toward the door, but Jonathan grabbed her again. Jackie still kicked and fought to get away from him. Somehow Jackie broke free from him and bolted towards the front door. When she opened up the door Mr. Lincoln was standing there. Jackie ran straight in his arms.

"Oh my God," panting, "You have to help me! He is trying to kill me. Terry please, baby, help me!"

Mr. Terry Lincoln pulled out his gun as he took Jackie and pushed her behind him. Mr. Lincoln looked over at Jackie as he raised a single finger to his lips.

Jonathan was still in the bedroom holding on to his head and rocking back and forth. He looked up in time to see Jackie and Mr. Terry Lincoln arriving right in front of him.

"Didn't I tell you that I was going to come back and kill you?"

Jonathan took in a deep breath and looked back up at the both of them. "So what now: You run and go and get your boy-toy to kill me?"

Mr. Lincoln looked down at Jonathan laughingly. "You really think I am her boy toy. Now, you see, I *was* her boyfriend... We needed you and Natalie to get out of the way so we can run our business like it is supposed to be run."

Jackie stepped from around Mr. Lincoln with a smile on her face. "I told you that I really didn't give two rats' asses about you or your children."

Jonathan just look at her and smiled.

"What the hell is so funny, Mr. Smith? I am about to kill your ass..."

Jonathan was still looking up at her as he got up off the floor. "Not if your boy-toy doesn't kill you first."

Jackie turned around. Mr. Lincoln had the gun pointed right at Jackie's stomach. She slowly backed up. "Wait! What the hell are you doing Terry? Are you crazy? I thought you said you love me..."

Mr. Lincoln added, "I wanted a fifty percent share of the business. I really did love your ass. This whole entire time you thought I love you," Mr. Lincoln advanced a little chuckled, "but girl, you are a waste of my time. What the hell do I look like? Being with someone as ratchet and ghetto as you!?"

With the gun still pointed at her, Jackie put her hands up. "OKay look, I will give *eighty percent* share of my business. Please just don't kill me, Mr. Lincoln!"

Terry Lincoln smiled. "I love when women start begging and pleading for their lives." Both gentlemen looked at each other and began to laugh.

"OKay Terry, don't sit up here and take too damn long on killing this bitch," Jonathan was still holding on to his head, "I have things to do." A moment later he realized Mr. Lincoln was hesitating to kill Jackie.

Terry now pleaded at Jonathan, "Hey man, do we really have to kill her? I mean she is the love of my life..."

Jonathan lowered his hands revealing his frown. "OKay, and you're saying this because... Hell, she was also my wife, but do you see me crying over spilled milk – her toxic ass? No! So if I was you, I would go ahead and kill her like I asked you to." Jonathan confidently walked out the room.

Lincoln walked a little closer to Jackie. "You know I don't want to do this, but you have to die." Jackie sprung on him, however, and she and Terry Lincoln began to fight over the gun.

When suddenly two shots had gone off Jonathan stopped in the dining room. He turned his head to look at the ceiling and smiled. "So I guess you got rid of our problem, right?!" he called out.

Jackie walked into the room towards Jonathan pointing Terry's gun at his back. "No! But I am about to get rid of your ass."

Jonathan turned around with a shocked look, "Wait! What the hell is going on? I told his dumb ass to kill you... Now look, his dumb ass couldn't even do that right!" Jonathan smiled at Jackie. "Well, they don't call you Lady James for nothing..."

Jackie looked at Jonathan and rolled her eyes. "I don't give two-" but before she could even finish her sentence Natalie strode into the room.

"Yeah, yeah – we know: you don't give a two rats' asses about this family, Jackie James. Or shall I say 'Lady James'?" Natalie smiled back at both of her parents. "But I will say this: you are a hard bitch to kill. I'll give you that much." Natalie walked around both of her parents while still smiling and looking them up and down. "Well, you did tell me that the next time I wanted to play cards I know where to find you. Well, bitch," Natalie held out her arms, "I found your black ass. Now how about we go ahead and play them cards?"

Jackie looked at Jonathan then back at Natalie. "Oh, I would love to play. After I whip your ass you're going to wish you never knew me as your mother."

"Oh bitch, let's get the playing then." Both of them raised their guns and started shooting at one another.

Natalie looked over when she caught sight that Mr. Lincoln was heading toward her way. "Oh shit. I see you bring back up!"

Natalie giggled. "That's nice, your boy-toy is here. Now the both of you can die together." They continued to shoot at one another.

Jonathan eased his way over to where Mr. Lincoln then stood, and he tapped him on the shoulder. "Well If you don't mind, how about we go ahead and finish what we had started?"

Mr. Lincoln turned around and looked back over at Jonathan. "It will be my pleasure to give you that ass whooping you have been asking for."

Jonathan drew his gun thinking Terry Lincoln was already as good as dead. Mr. Lincoln took out his gun and pointed at Jonathan, but before he could even fire it Charlette Diamond walked into the room. She pulled out her gun and fired it up into the ceiling.

"What the hell is going on here? I leave for five minutes and you are at each other's throats! Now, like I said before, you have started acting-" However before she could finish, Natalie jumped in and cut Charlette off.

"Look lil' girl, don't you have a doll to play with or a jump rope game or something? This is not what you really want to get into."

Charlette glared at Natalie. "Look, woman, I know you're supposed to be the baddest gang bitch on the street, but there is a new baddest bitch, and her name is Charlette Diamond. Now if you don't mind I would like to talk to my Grandparents about half of my share of the business."

Natalie looked back over at her parents then back at Charlette. With a frown Natalie exclaimed, "Bitch, you have no idea who the hell you are fucking with do you?" Natalie reached for Charlette's throat, wrapping her hands around it so tight that the niece couldn't even barely breathe.

Jackie ran over toward Natalie and Charlette. "Get your hand off of her!" However the more Jackie tried to pull Natalie's hands, the tighter they got. Finally, Natalie let Charlette go.

"The next time you want to go up against me, lil' girl, your young ass better think about it!" Charlette looked up at Natalie, still holding on to her neck and trying to gasp for air. Natalie stood over Charlette once more and bent down to whisper, "Stop fucking playing with me." Natalie straightened up and looked at the rest of the family. "And that went for the rest of you who keep on doubting me. Like I said before," Natalie jabbed a finger at her mother, Jackie, "I am not the one to be played with."

Natalie turned around and walked away.

Chapter 26

Charlette had come running behind Natalie. "Who the hell do you think you are talking to like that?"

Natalie stopped at the doorway, turned around, looked at Charlotte and laughed. "Lil' girl, please! I have told you one time before. You really do not want to get into a fight with me. Now back the hell off before I kill your little young ass."

Charlette watched Natalie walk away. Natalie's cell phone rang with an unlisted phone number. She looked down at it, and frowned. "Hello, who is this?" However, with no reply coming, Natalie just kept repeating herself. Natalie looked out the car window thinking once again, 'I wonder if that was that bitch ass sister of mine, Jessica. I wonder if that was her trying to call and has hidden her number,' Natalie smiled, 'Well we are just going to see about that now – won't we?' She took in a deep breath, 'OKay Nat! Now how am I going to find this so-called sister of mine?' Natalie felt herself getting excited about killing her sister. 'Well, you can't go home to your beautiful condo – your little rat-ugly-ass sister destroyed it. Thank God I have a penthouse in Richmond.'

Natalie pulled up to the building that held that penthouse. She noticed that a black sedan was sitting in her driveway. Natalie looked around before she got out of her own car. Natalie whispered aloud, "What the hell? And whose is this car sitting in my damn driveway?" She reached into her pocket book and pulled out her 9mm. "OKay, since I don't know who the hell you are. Let's see if you'll tell my friend Pinky, here." When Natalie got closer to the car the door opened. She aimed and commanded, "Alright don't come any closer. Let me see your hands," as if she was a police officer.

"We already know that Natalie James can't get along with the po-po," Ryan stepped out of the car with his hands up slightly in front of him.

"Boy, you almost caught a bullet in the head. You know I'm crazy as hell with cars I don't know."

Ryan stepped clear of the car, and he growled in a low voice, "Yeah don't I know that."

Natalie stared back over at him. "Excuse me, did you say something Ryan?"

Ryan perked up into a smile. "Nope, my dear, I didn't say not one word."

Natalie scowled as her eyebrow went up. "OKay well... I want to know how the hell did you know where I live? Are you working for that damn sister of mind too? Because if you are, I will kill you right here and right now."

Ryan chuckled and replied, "Girl, I won't dare work for that delusional bitch. What kinda person do you think I am?"

Natalie kept Ryan a straight face. "I don't know, but I do know this; I am going to need your help killing both her and my mother.

Ryan did a double take to face Natalie. One would have thought someone was after him. "Come again? You need me to do what? I just know you didn't say you need me to help you kill your mother and that crazy bitch sister of yours."

Natalie walked into the house. She stopped and turned around and smiled. "Yep, that is exactly what I just said."

Ryan put a hand on his forehead as he shook it. "Oh, my God! I am going to die tonight trying to help you take down the most dangerous woman in the city."

Natalie looked back at Ryan and pressed her lips into a pout. "Will you get a hold of yourself? I am not going to let no one harm you," then in her low tone voice, "well I mean they might get a bullet or two in, but they are not going to kill you. I'll made sure of that. OKay?" She patted Ryan on his back, smiled and added, "Now let's get clean up and go and take down some James gremlins."

Ryan threw his hands up into the air. "Yep! I am dead. Long gone."

Then Natalie's phone rang again. She stopped and turned back around to look at Ryan, then down at her phone again if she was confused about the call. Natalie picked up the phone and answered it. "Hello!" It was Jessica on the other end.

"Yeah! What's taking your ass so long? I thought you wanted a piece of me. Apparently you do want to get your ass beat by your little sister."

Natalie took the Phone away from her ear. "What the hell do you mean? I don't want no ass beat, girl. Apparently you don't really know who the hell I am! Do you Miss Jessica James?"

Jessica laughed through the phone. "Oh, I know you can't beat me, Nat, you never could. Even when we were children you couldn't beat me. So why don't you just admit that I'm the best at everything."

Natalie took the phone away from her ear again and stared at it hard. This time Natalie pushed the dial button to hang up the phone. "That bitch got the nerve to say I can't beat her little black ass. Well, we will just see about that." Natalie kept on babbling on and on.

Ryan yelled into the bedroom" Look, Nat, we all know you can beat her. So why are you letting her get to you like that?"

Natalie peeked out of the bedroom, and she give Ryan the evil eye. "What the hell did you just say to me? I already know that I can beat her, but I want her scrawny little ass to know it, too."

Natalie finished getting dressed at the same time that there was a knock at the front door. Natalie frowned as she looked back at Ryan. They both took out their guns. She walked a little closer to the door. "Who is it?" But no voice from the other side replied. "I said who is it, damn it?" Natalie got upset because no one would say anything back. Natalie opened up the door and Charlette Diamond was standing there with a grin on her face.

"Surprised?! Happy to see me auntie?!"

Natalie gaped and just stared. "Hell naw! I am not happy to see your ass. How the hell did you know where I stay? Did your yellow ass follow me?"

Charlette held her head down. "For you to know, no, I didn't follow your ass. Grandpa told me where you stay so I decided to come and give you a visit. So here I am."

Natalie looked over at Ryan then back at Charlette. "Look, I can't be bothered with you right now. I am a little bit busy, OKay?"

Charlette continued to smile. "Busy like how, killing grandpa and grandma? Hell, I can help with that part."

"Girl, what the hell has gotten into you? You really want to be into the family business that bad?"

Charlette walked over a little closer to where Natalie was standing. "Yes I really want to be into the family business. Not only do I want to be in the family business, but I want what's mine."

"...and what the hell is that, money?"

Charlette cheerily replied, "No, I want powder and authority."

Natalie leaned her head and snidely laughed. "Bitch, get out of here with that mess. You will be waiting a long damn time for that to happen. Look, as far as the family business goes, you're gonna have to take down the queen herself." Natalie held onto her stomach with her mocking laughing. "Well, I'm going to take a shower. You can wait if you like." Natalie looked back at Charlette and lowered and shook her head. "Oh my God, this heifer really thinks she is going to get some authority. Yeah, right. Authority my ass..."

After Natalie finished up with her bath she decided to go and visit her sister Dakota. 'Lord please help me just as well as you are helping my sister, Dakota."

Natalie walked into the hospital atrium to find Jessica sitting in a chair waiting for her. "What the hell are you doing here? Who told you to be here? You just tried to kill her not too long ago."

Jessica got up from her chair, and she walked over as if she was walking to be a Miss Top Model. "I chose to be here, and yes what I did to our older sibling was wrong of me, Natalie."

Natalie scanned around the hospital lobby. "I am sorry, but was your ass talking to me? I mean I just want to make sure, because this doesn't sound like the Jessica James that I know."

Jessica looked Natalie over and smiled. "Little Natalie, there are a lot of things that you really don't know about me."

Natalie leaned her head to the side and frowned. "Yeah bitch, I don't know... but this is what I want to know: Why the hell you want to kill me?

Jessica walked away, but then stopped and turned around. "Because I don't like you bitch!" Jessica pulled her gun and shot at Natalie.

"What the hell?" Natalie dove over by the sofa. 'I knew this bitch was crazy, but damn! She has got to be toxic also?' Natalie fired back, but upon emerging from cover there was no sign of Jessica anywhere.

Chapter 27

Natalie got up off the floor still expecting her sister to be anywhere. 'I can't believe this heifer took a shot at me in the damn hospital. What is with everyone in this family, and, why the hell do they want me dead so damn much? This is it. I am not going to take it easy on anybody else.' Natalie ran into her sister Dakota's room to make sure Jessica was not in there. 'You lucky bitch. I am going to make sure that I find you, and I will kill you. Mark my word your day is coming.' Natalie ran back to her car and dialed Charlette's Number.

"Hello, what's up auntie? What can I do for you?"

Natalie was so discouraged, however, that she couldn't even think or talk. Natalie threw her phone onto the seat beside her. 'Damn! Now she can't make out what I am trying to say.' Natalie tried to re-call Charlette's phone, but this time it went straight to voicemail. "Oh my God! What in the hell is going on? Girl, you need to pick your phone." On a third try she got no answer.

Natalie pulled into her driveway and noticed that her front door was open. She got out of her car slowly. Natalie pulled out her gun and crept up the walkway. "Hey Charlette, hey girl, where you at?" She thought to yell out Ryan's name he also didn't answer. Should she call out the both of them. It seemed strange to Natalie that they would leave her door laying open. She walked inside of the house, and suddenly Ryan pulled her by both her arms, knocking the gun out of her hand. Natalie went stumbling over to the sofa. "What the hell is wrong with you boy? Have you lost your damn mind?"

AS if in answer, Ryan looked at Natalie and laughed, then he pushed Charlette's back so hard that she ended up falling on the floor.

"Now I have both of you bitches right where I want you at! It's time for you two ladies to know the truth." Ryan turned his head over to them and smiled.

Charlette and Natalie looked at one another. "Do you really think that Jessica and my mother are going to give you a piece of the shared business?" Natalie laughed, "I should have known something was fishy about your short ass. You will get what's-" but before Natalie could finish her sentence Ryan had cut her off with pointed finger.

"I'm going to need the both of you to shut the hell up!"

Charlette smoldered as she looked at Ryan as if she wanted to smack the taste out of his mouth. "Excuse me! Who the hell are you talking to? You really have forgotten who you are dealing with, chunk." Charlette stood up while waving her hand at Ryan's face, he took one step back to glower at both of them.

"Y'all really think the both of you can take me on?"

"I'll tell you what," Natalie got up off the sofa, "come a little closer and I will show you how bad I really am."

Ryan kept the gun pointed at them when a sudden knock came at the front door. Natalie looked over at Charlette, then back at Ryan. "Are you expecting any company?" Ryan's face looked surprised and a little worried. The knock came again a little louder.

He turned around, commanding as he walked towards the front door, "You better not say one word!" to which Natalie and Charlette leaned their heads and folded their arms. Ryan opened the front door.

Suddenly Natalie jumped up and yelled out, "He has a gun, help us!"

Ryan slammed the door and locked it. "I thought I told neither one of you to made a sound."

Natalie beheld Ryan with one eyebrow high. "And who the hell's supposed to listen to your little short ass. You know I am really getting tired of your mess." Natalie smacked Ryan across his face.

The gun dropped out of Ryan's hands, and Charlette jumped up, grabbed it and pointed it at him.

"Give me a reason to shoot your little, short ass." Ryan held out his hand and begged for mercy. Mid-sentence on begging forgiveness Natalie walk over to Charlette, took the gun out of her hands and shot Ryan dead into his face.

She turned back at Charlotte looking as if she didn't give two rats' asses if she'd shot him or not. "You were taking too long for me. Next time someone holds a gun at your head and doesn't shoot, please make sure that I am not around. The next time it may be you or it may be them not making it out of here."

Charlette looked down at Ryan then back up at Natalie. "I never liked his butt in any way."

Natalie glanced back down at Ryan's dead body. "Neither did I. Now come on, you gotta help me kill your grandma, and your nasty ass Aunt Jessica."

Later on that afternoon Natalie and Charlette showed up back over Mr. Lincoln's house. Charlette asked, "OKay and again, why the hell are we here?"

Natalie rolled her eyes. "Girl, if you don't pay attend to what's about to go down I am going to kill you myself."

Charlotte frowned. "You better hope that I don't kill you first auntie."

They continued to go back and forth until Mr. Lincoln emerged from the house. Natalie put her hand towards Charlette's face to tell her to pause the conversation.

"I beg your pardon? Can you get your damn hand out of my face?"

Natalie went to say something about Mr. Lincoln, but got distracted by Charlette 's smart mouthed comment.

She snapped her head around and looked at her niece. "What the hell did you just say to me?"

Charlette smiled and turned her head towards the window. "So are we going in there or what?" With her hands out towards Natalie showing that she really wanted to know what was the plan?

"Oh, we are going right up in there." They both began to get out of the car. Natalie reached behind her and pulled out her pink 9mm.

Charlette looked at her wide-eyed. "What in the hell are you doing with that?" She was still looking at Natalie confused. "Who the hell are you about to kill?"

Natalie crept a little closer to the house, but stopped and turned around and looked back at her. "I am about to kill your Grandma and auntie." Natalie had a look upon her face as if she had just won the lottery; Charlette leaned back and shook her head.

Natalie and Charlette stormed into the house gangbusters style. Jackie jumped up from her seat and turn on Natalie.

"What the hell is your problem girl?!"

Natalie did walked toward her mother and smiled. "You know exactly what's my problem, mother Jackie. I want to know where the hell Jessica is."

Jackie smiled back and replied in the same sweet tone, "Why do you wish to know about your beloved sister?"

Charlette walked in front of the both them. "Are you crazy, or you just flat out crazy?"

Natalie pushed Charlette aside. "Like I said, where the hell is your daughter?" However, by this time Jessica was coming through the hallway.

"OKay, so I guess everyone is looking for me." Jessica entered the living room. "Oh hell! I thought I got rid of your red ass. Girl, what is it that you want? I mean damn, are you that obsessed with me or what?"

Natalie balked at Jessica, "Girl, please! Ain't nobody obsessed with your delusional ass. Now, what I can tell you is that I am about to kill your ass." Natalie leveled her gun and started firing.

Suddenly everyone in the living room started shooting at one another. Jackie aimed towards Natalie. "You really think that I am going to let you kill my baby girl? Bitch, you have another thing coming!"

Natalie backed up, with the gun still in her hand. "I always knew that she was your favorite, but after tonight she is going to be your least favorite daughter."

Jackie frowned. "What the hell are you talking about?"

"Natalie put her hands up in the air. "I thought you knew, mother, she wants to take over the family business; She wants you dead and gone."

Jackie looked over at Jessica and her frown deepened. "Jess, is this true? You want me dead so you can take over."

Jessica smirked. "Hell yeah, I want your ass dead! If I can get you and my daddy out of the way all this will be mine."

Jackie put her hands over her face, and tears came rolling down. She was shocked to learn that her baby girl, Jessica, had come to betray her.

"I can't believe that you would do this to me after all I have done for you and this family."

Jessica swiveled the gun to level it at Jackie, 'Well Bitch, believe, because after you are dead to me. This will all be mine." Jessica shot at her mother, but Charlette jumped between the both of them. "Dammit, this bitch just shot me!"

Jessica looked between her mother and Charlette. "Well I guess I just have to finish the job I started." She tried to fire at both of them when Natalie shot at Jessica. Jessica turned to look at Natalie. "Oh, so you want to be a part of the show, too, right...?"

Natalie replied, "You damn right, I want a piece of the show! This is why we are here, right little sister?"

Jessica looked at Natalie and slyly smiled. "Naw, I think I am going to wait until your big sister, Dakota, joins us again."

Natalie looked at Jessica and frowned. "And what the hell do you mean by that?"

Jessica walked towards the front door. She stopped and turned around and indicated Charlette. "I think you need to ask your niece about her mother's playing skills."

Natalie looked back towards Charlotte, then back at Jessica. "Oh, don't think you are going to get out of an ass whuppin' that fast..."

Jessica smiled, "Oh, don't worry, I will be looking forward to that ass whuppin'," then she walked out of the house.

LINDA STUDIO PRODUCTION

Linda Spence Howard

www.ingramcontent.com/pod-product-compliance
Lightning Source LLC
Chambersburg PA
CBHW050755250626

47155CB00005B/2082